five

Speccy ~~Four~~ Eyes

Speccy ~~Four~~ *five* Eyes

Alan Burgess Wilson

© Alan Burgess Wilson, 2018

Published by Alan Burgess Wilson

A CIP catalogue record for this book is available from the British Library.

ISBN 978-1-9996422-0-4

Book layout and design by Clare Brayshaw

Cover image © Mercava2007

Prepared and printed by:

York Publishing Services Ltd
64 Hallfield Road
Layerthorpe
York YO31 7ZQ

Tel: 01904 431213

Website: www.yps-publishing.co.uk

Chapter 1

9th June 1998

The little cottage was basic, with minimal furniture – but was adequate. It was a mid-terrace, pretending to be a Cheshire black and white cottage, with tiny patches of grass front and back. The front door opened into the living room, off which there was a bathroom to one side, and stairs to two small bedrooms on the other. To the rear was a kitchen, without a door between it and the living room; at the end of this, there was the back door.

It was a gloriously sunny spring morning; I was happily retired at 53, and free, almost single, and had what was left of life to look forward to, whatever that was. I had been given the 'all clear'; my cancer had gone. I was sitting on a dining room chair at my improvised desk, which was half under the stairs, about where the kitchen/living room door should have been. The spreadsheet that I was playing with listed all my expenditure from the current account, still jointly held by me and my 'soon to be' ex-wife.

I had put a curtain over the partly glass, back door, both to keep out drafts, and for privacy, because anyone at that door could see anyone at the other door, if you see what I mean.

A slight movement at the back door curtain, almost a darkening, drew my eye down the side of the curtain where there was a bit of a gap. Leaning back as far as I could on the chair, to almost tipping point, I waited to see if it was going to reoccur, if it would result in a knock, or was simply the draft that I had attempted to keep at bay.

With legs and arms flailing, I only just managed to get four chair legs back on the floor, as the knock on the front door made me jump. Not that it was a loud knock, but certainly an unexpected one. Still looking over my shoulder at the back door, and, catching another glimpse of a movement, I looked through the front window to see the dark suited figure – the knocking culprit. He raised his hand to knock again, but stopped as he saw the movement in the window, and met my gaze. Without a smile, he indicated, with a very slight head movement, towards the door that he clearly expected to be opened.

"Good morning. Is it Mr Burgess? Sam Burgess?"

With a high degree of trepidation, I said a long, drawn-out, 'Yeess'.

"I'm Detective Inspector Maynard; could we have a chat…" pause, "Inside, please?" Stepping back, it was obvious that it was more of an instruction than a request, which clearly did not have a negative response option. I retreated into the living room, pursued by him and the closing door.

"Perhaps you would be good enough to let my colleague in. He's waiting at the back door." Again, an instruction not a request. I opened the back door to be confronted by a smiling, friendly looking, casually dressed man of about 30.

"Hi Sam, I'm DC Williams. Take a seat". Another gesticulation with the head towards the living room, and I retreated, and sat opposite the suit, the two of us occupying my only two easy chairs.

"OK, gents, what have I done to deserve such a visit. It's clearly not a parking offence, is it?".

"No Sam, I'm afraid not. Could you tell me what your movements were yesterday from, say, lunchtime until midnight?" DI Maynard, taking the lead, continued: "You don't mind if my colleague has a look around whilst we chat?" He nodded at the DC, assuming my agreement.

"I don't suppose you would like to tell me what this is about?" I asked.

"No, but what I will tell you is that it is important that you tell me what I need to know, and then I will explain fully. So... yesterday, then?"

"Well, I nipped into town at about 1 o'clock, did a bit of shopping, and got back probably half 2ish, cut the grass, painted for a couple of hours – I'm a bit of an amateur artist, (oils), cooked, had a bottle of red... watched a bit of telly, and went to bed about 10ish. That's about it really."

"Did you meet anyone you know in town? Talk to anyone? Anyone see you come and go?"

"No, and I doubt if anyone in the shops that I visited would remember me either."

"So, what did you buy?"

"Food; some steak for dinner, frozen stuff, oh yes, and a couple of books from the charity shop." The heavy mob returned from upstairs, and exchanged looks with the suit with a very slight, almost imperceptible shake of the head, which I took to mean 'nothing found'.

"Come on, what's this about?"

Ignoring the question, he continued: "When did you last see your wife?"

"About the middle of last week. No, that's wrong; it was the day before yesterday; I called on my way back from my Mother's to ask if I could get some of my things out of the garage."

"And did you discuss anything else with her?"

"Not really, we talked a bit about money; when we split up, she had emptied the bank account, but it had been a bit of a knee-jerk reaction on her part, and she had paid it all back in. We have agreed to keep the joint account going until everything is settled, and I had agreed to limit my withdrawals to just essential living expenses."

"That sounds very civilised. Have relations between you not been, well, strained?"

"Strained is not the word I would use; it's been like the third bloody world war for the last few months, but she has slowly begun to recover, but will never forgive me."

"Forgive you for what?"

"I had an affair which... er... 'came to light', shall we say. Then I left, or to be more truthful, she threw me out with a bin bag full of clothes." There was a pause, a long pause; clearly thinking time.

"Sam, I'm afraid your wife was found dead on the kitchen floor of her home this morning, and the circumstances are such that we believe that she didn't die of natural causes. We have a witness who says that you were at the house yesterday afternoon. Do you have anything to say about that?"

"No, I wasn't there yesterday. How do I prove that I wasn't there? I don't know. All I can say is that I wasn't.

I don't believe this is real. Jane is dead? Really? Dead? Are you saying she's been killed? This is sleepy rural Cheshire, things like this don't happen here. Jane is dead? Do the children know? Where are the dogs? Who is looking after the dogs? Sorry, I'm in shock. Why am I talking about the fucking dogs?"

"Calm down, Sam, I know this is a shock, or, at least, I hope it's a shock but..." He let the question hang there for a minute, and then: "I have to tell you that Jane was shot at close range with a small calibre weapon, probably silenced, and, I'm sorry... but, so too were the dogs." There was a pause, my mind was in turmoil, a thousand things went through it in a split second, and I can't remember any of them. I was brought back to reality with a crash. "We need to do some forensics to enable us to eliminate you from our enquiries – gun shot residue, prints, that sort of thing, and would like you to come to the station with us, please, if you would, now." Another 'no negative' option, I thought.

"Yeah! Sure, no problem. I don't believe this: Jane shot and killed, the dogs – I loved those dogs." I stopped dead, and realised what I had said. There was no point trying to retract or diminish it, so I decided to just let it lay. "Can I phone my brother in law? I just need someone to know what is happening, and I need to know that someone will be with my mother, 'cos she is 90, fighting fit, but this will be a real shock to her; she is very fond of Jane. Oh my god, I mean she *was* fond of Jane. I just can't believe this is happening."

"Sam, you can ring him when we get to the station. You are not under arrest; you are not being cautioned. We merely wish to eliminate you from the enquiries that we obviously need to make."

"Yeh! Right. Er... I'll get some stuff together then."

"You don't need anything, Sam; we won't need to keep you for long. Do you have any goldfish to feed, a cat to put out, anyone due to visit?"

"No, I guess not." We all stood, and I locked the front door, and we left through the back, where there was an unmarked (to my relief), police car. Doris, my 80 something next-door neighbour, would have gossiped about it for weeks. It never occurred to me, at that stage that, when it all became public knowledge, I would be the centre of media attention anyway. Outside, I was hit by the smell of freshly cut grass, bees buzzing about their morning commute, sun beginning to fire-up for the summer: 'What a lovely day to get carted off to the nick,' I thought, cynically. I locked the door.

"Oh! By the way, Sam, did Jane say anything to you about selling-up, leaving, moving on, packing stuff up, anything like that?"

"No, not that I can remember; she always said that, no matter what, she wanted to stay in the house she loved with the dogs. I had always agreed that I would leave without causing her problems, financial or otherwise. Bloody hell, I even said that I would leave the dogs with her!"

"Can you explain why there would be a box in the kitchen, packed, as if preparing to vacate?"

"Hang on, what the hell does 'preparing to vacate' mean?"

"Well ok, why do you think a box of crockery, you know, cups, saucers, plates, in fact a complete dinner service, would be packed in a cardboard box, and left in the middle of the kitchen floor? Was that some sort of message you were trying to send, Sam?" I stopped dead. It felt like I'd been hit by a truck, dazed and momentarily 'off-balance'. I realised that my mouth was wide open like someone in deep shock, which I was.

In a very strange contradictory way, DI Maynard reached out and took my elbow, showing surprising concern and almost kindness. 'Strange gesture', I thought later.

It was as I was led in a daze to the car that I realised how deep the shit was that I had just jumped into – or had been pushed into….and I knew the significance of a box of crockery.

Chapter 2

10th June 1998

It was all a bit of a blur really – the custody, the interrogation, the repeated questions, and my deepening conviction that I was not being believed. I knew that they were convinced that they had their man. Come on, why else would a respected, clean-living teacher and housewife be shot in her own home? Why else than if it wasn't a crime of passion, perpetrated by a sad, bitter, twisted 'ex', who stood to gain from the demise of his partner, who held title to half the house, goods, chattels and all the bollocks. Except that, (a) it wasn't true, and (b), I knew the truth. So…why not just tell them the truth? Well, because the truth was even more unbelievable than the conclusion they had reached.

Left in an interrogation room for hours, I had a lot of thinking time between 'sessions'. I knew they had to charge me at some stage, or let me go, and I also knew that when they did (let me go), I would have to deal with the other issues that had yet to surface. I also knew that whilst I was locked up (albeit 'helping with enquiries'), I was at least protected from any other 'interested parties'. My priority was to get out of the lock-up. I couldn't do anything whilst 'in the nick', so I played the game and waited. At some point they had to let me go, but I knew that I would be followed and watched until I did something that would implicate or incriminate me.

After that afternoon, the night and all the next day, I was allowed to leave, with a caution, of course, about not leaving the area, an officious, "We will still need to talk to you, Sir", and an 'off the record': "Don't think you'll get away with this, you bastard".

I went home (on the bus), joining the tired, incommunicative commuters who were all heading home, unaware that their fellow passenger was a suspected murderer. I was lost in my own thoughts, and remember little of the journey. Walking the last few hundred yards from the bus stop, I was blasted back to reality by the horn of the truck that I was about to step in front of. I walked down the side of the cottages, past an overflowing bin, stepping around the rubbish that had accumulated. The parking area at the back was empty, except for my car – everything just as I'd left it. Life on the surface was 'normal', but my heart rate told another story. Closing the gate, I admired my postage stamp sized lawn, neatly mowed; I'd even managed to get stripes.

It was strangely comforting to enter my little kitchen, close the door, draw the curtain across, and lean back against it, taking several deep breaths. I stood there for a long time and watched the traffic flash past the living room window. With a big sigh, I collected a glass from the draining board, a bottle from the rack, and went into the living room. I don't know how long I sat for, but was suddenly aware that it had gone dark – street lights lit the room with that yellowy glow. I looked through the window at the passing traffic and the normality of village life, and, with a sigh, drew the curtains on the outside world.

The bottle was half empty (definitely not half full). I thought about how my past had caught up with me, the mess I was in, and wondered how I could extricate myself from it. I had tried to think of the options, unsure of what to do next. I needed to talk to someone – who? What the hell do I say to them, anyway? I was beginning to feel sorry for myself and needed to pull myself together. 'Come on, get a grip; you can deal with this. Sort yourself out.' It was a spur of the moment decision really; I got in the car and drove, via a meandering route, back towards my old house that I had shared with Jane.

I watched the rear-view mirror all the way (narrowly missing several parked cars and lamp posts), to see if I was being followed. I didn't spot anything – the roads were quiet, and I stopped in the Late Shop car park to think for a while, and watched the traffic and shoppers coming and going. It felt a bit too public, and a bit too well lit. I wanted to be inconspicuous, so I drove on, and then stopped again in a lay-by, which felt better.

It was getting late; I did a drive-by of the house, went all around the village, did another drive-by, and then turned into the pub car park that was four houses down from my (Jane's now), house. There was a police car parked outside the house; all was dark – the house, the car and the street, but I couldn't see if anyone was in the car parked under the trees. I assumed that there was. It was now approaching closing time, but there was no-one in the car park, just three parked cars. I parked in the darkest corner, and got out. There was low music noise, and, occasionally, loud laughter coming from the open rear door of the pub. I got out of the car, and walked to the end of the car park, to the rear wall of the pub, and waited for the security lights to time out.

As my eyes adjusted to the darkness, I felt my way into the beer garden, and, carefully, moved a bench to the side wall of the next-door garden; I stood on the bench, and eased myself over the wall. There was a drop of a few feet to the ground, and I mentally apologised for trampling on whatever the vegetation was that I had landed on. I stood still in the black shadow of the wall, and listened. No sounds of life, and no indication that I had disturbed anyone. Looking around, a yard or so down the garden, I saw a wheelbarrow leaning against the wall. I carefully moved it to mark my position at the wall for the return trip, and upended it, so that I could climb on it and scramble back over the wall later.

All the gardens were the same length and width until Jane's, which was double the width of the others. I think the builder had intended to add another house at some stage, but never got around to it. We had bought it at the right time, and the double width had been a major plus in the purchase decision. One of the first things we/I did in the garden was to put up a large shed right at the bottom, well away from the house and the drive, and then built a detached garage between the road and the garden. The gardens between the pub and my garden shed were separated by low hedges and bits of fencing, with no uniformity at all.

Moving slowly, negotiating the various obstacles, I crept through paths, lawns and flower beds, climbing over and fighting my way through hedges and over bits of netting, and, in one place, an ivy-covered trellis which almost fell apart as I scrambled over it. I paused, and tried to slow my breathing to listen for sounds of movement or activity. It was still quiet, and I wondered if anyone other than me would have been able to hear the pounding in my chest: 'Calm down, calm down, you've been in tighter spots than this; get a grip, man'. The last hedge was a bit more of a problem – too high and too thick, but I remembered a gap that I had had to fill in to make the garden dog proof. It looked different from this side, and it took me a while of careful exploration to find it. Pushing the netting and posts in front of me, I squeezed through, and was twenty feet and two apple trees from the shed door.

The combination padlock opened easily, once I had managed to get the tumblers to line up with the 1066 code. I hung the lock in the hasp, opened the door, slowly lifting slightly, because I knew it would make a horrendous scraping noise if I wasn't careful. This was going to be the difficult bit. Feeling my way carefully in the dark, around the pots, tools and lawnmowers (why the hell did I have three of them, anyway, must be a man thing), I fought my way to the back of the shed to the re-cycled wardrobe with double drawers at the bottom. I had to move bags of compost, plastic containers of weed stuff, kill stuff, and grow quicker stuff, out of the way so that I could open the drawer. This was far more than normal access, because I had to actually take the drawer out. I didn't want the contents; I wanted the Petticoat Tails Shortbread Biscuit tin that was in the hole in the floor, cut out specially to contain it. I didn't want to be trying to negotiate the hedges and fences carrying the tin, so I removed the bundle, and the small box, stuffed them into the inside pockets of my black fleece jacket, and put everything back as it was.

Pushing the drawer back, I froze, as the rake fell from its nail on the wall with a crash as it hit a mower, and then another crash, as it hit the floor, and then the wall.

Leaving it where it landed, I got to the door as quickly as I could, and listened again. 'Should I just run? Would the copper at the front be on his way to investigate?' I listened, waited… heart pounding again.

It occurred to me that, only a few days earlier, the dogs would have been going mad; no one would still be asleep.

Locking the door again, I retraced my steps, this time, with a little less caution, I just wanted to get away and home to the comparative safety of my little cottage. The undignified scramble back over the wall left me panting and breathless: 'Not young enough for this game, anymore', I thought, but I could still remember the basic rules of hide and seek. The pub door was closed now, but still had customers for the 'lock-in'. I eased, carefully, out of the car park, hoping that the copper was charged with staying at his post, rather than pursuing a prospective drink-drive suspect leaving a pub car park after closing time. It was all as it had been when I'd arrived, and I drove on – still no interest, still not followed.

Back to the cottage, and I drove as slowly as I dared, not wanting to draw attention. I looked in all the parked cars as I passed them, all seemed empty, and there were none I didn't recognise. As I turned into the narrow entrance, a movement inside a black Audi parked at the junction ten yards ahead caught my eye. I was committed to the turn, and didn't have chance to look for long enough to be sure, but it looked like someone had ducked down in the seat as I had approached. I parked in my usual space, got out, and, with the clunk and flash of central locking, went into the house.

It didn't feel quite right – nothing I could put my finger on, just a feeling. Locking the door behind me, I explored every room on the way upstairs. Then, with the light off, I opened the bedroom curtain, slowly, just enough to look up the road – and the Audi was still there. I checked all the rooms again on the way down. Retrieving the half bottle of red and my glass, I drew the curtains in the kitchen, over the back door, poured a glass, and sat at the kitchen table, putting the bundle and box in front of me; I unwrapped it.

A flood of memories came with the bundle – faces, places, incidents, and, I'll admit, to fear, to being scared, to being frightened by both the past and the future.

Chapter 3

July 1968

Looking back now, as a seventeen-year-old, it was a tremendously brave thing to do. I had joined the Army in 1962, to get away from my Victorian, bullying father. This was after the end of Conscription; I signed up for nine years, but served for ten, because I should have been eighteen. After basic training in Oswestry, a short posting to Shoeburyness in Essex, then Germany, back to Salisbury, Malaysia, my regiment arrived in Weeton, an ex RAF Camp near Blackpool (of all places).

Life was full of fun, beer, kiss-me-quick hats, and a generally carefree non-combatant (but military) existence. We were a very close-knit group of about 10 who shared everything together, even women. We drank a lot, and got into all sorts of mischief. Buy me enough beer, and I'll tell you who killed the Regimental Ceremonial Goose, who ate it for Christmas Dinner, and who set fire to the Battery Office. Bad language was the norm, and we certainly lived up to the 'swears like a trooper' description. Strangely though, we did not, in those days, swear in front of a lady – not even those who were not ladies. It seems to be the norm now, sadly, most modern ladies with the same vocabulary.

At that time, I was one of the very few who owned a vehicle. This made me quite popular, and the gang went everywhere in my Commer van, which I can only describe as an earlier version of the Ford Transit that we all now know. Although it had doors at the back and a passenger door, only the sliding driver's door opened. We would drive with this door open, and, upon arrival at our destination, everyone would climb over the engine cover and scramble out over the top of me (the driver), before I had chance to apply brakes, select neutral or stop the engine. This became a ritual and happened everywhere we went.

Because it had no seats in the back (just a mattress), it was also considered good fun to all rush to one side of the van as we went around a bend, to see if we could get round on two wheels. Not sure how we managed not to turn it over.

It was in the summer of '68 that one of the gang, who was in the Army Air Corps, had an RAF mate who suggested that he might be able to 'arrange' a trip from Brizenorton to Kenya. There was a regular flight out and back every week to Mombassa, and, if we volunteered to hump the cargo on and off, we could hitch a lift and stay for a week, do the safari stuff, and come back again the week after. This was considered the trip of a lifetime; never again would we get such an opportunity.

The trip was duly sanctioned, signed off as a training exercise, and we rushed around making last minute arrangements for the trip – injections updated, packing etc. My last-minute stuff included the purchase of a very large telephoto camera lens, which cost almost a year's wages. I had been a fairly serious photographer for some years, and had bought an expensive (but cheap out there) 35m Nikon SLR camera when I was in Malaya.

The trip was the only topic of conversation for the few weeks prior to leaving. It was devastating to be told two days before departure: 'Sorry guys; your trip's off, we're going to Ireland.'

All Safari thoughts gone, we were shipped (literally), via Liverpool to Northern Ireland in days. In a whirlwind of activity, we were thrown into the chaos of Londonderry at the height of 'the troubles'.

It was a strange existence: 4 hours on, 4 hours off. On the streets day and night, being locked up in a fortress-like compound in Ballykelly when we were off duty. It was a bit like being in prison, and we actually looked forward to getting out on the streets, even though it was terrifying.

I don't consider myself to be brave, and openly admit to being scared shitless in some of the situations we were in. I remember a story that my mother used to tell about how brave her son is (or should that be 'was'). I was about twelve or thirteen when our little scruffy mongrel dog was set upon in our garden by a much larger dog that had 'strayed' up our drive. I rushed out of the house and grabbed them both, pulling them apart amidst all the fangs, slobber, snot and snarls (and that was just mother). This wasn't bravery mother; it was stupidity. My bravery amounts to not thinking too much about the consequences – not seeing the dangers.

When off duty, we listened to News Bulletins, talked to RUC colleagues, and generally kept up to speed with what was happening in other areas, and in particular Belfast. We usually found that what kicked off in Belfast, kicked off in 'Derry within a few hours. Patrols around the streets were okish; just the occasional abuse and spitting, but the locals seemed to cope with it (only joking).

We had a couple of permanently manned OPs (observation posts) overlooking key trouble spots. One of them was a commandeered penthouse flat on the top floor of a tower block overlooking Free Derry Corner on one side, with panoramic views of various parts of the city on the other. It was to here that I started taking my camera, and realised what an asset to our surveillance my long lens could be. It was a fantastic piece of kit, and I could see stuff that binoculars couldn't, and could 'capture' the image too.

Chapter 4

August 1968

One Friday evening, it all began to kick-off at various points around the city, and our patrol got a call on the radio asking if the guy with the big lens could be 'borrowed' to photograph some particularly troublesome people – so off I went. Poor light made things difficult, as did camera shake, caused mainly by fear, and the things thrown at us – bricks, broken paving slabs, roof tiles, bottles (sometimes full of petrol, never beer, but mainly piss), darts, potatoes with razor blades in them – the list goes on. At that time, years before Digital, I used Ilford HP4, black and white film, 400ASA, but I up-rated it to 800. It was then that I stopped seeing the results; some would have been good, but a lot would have been un-usable. After that night, it became a regular thing, and I was rushed around from site to site photographing as many trouble makers as I could. I was asked to try and get pictures of the ringleaders; this was always difficult, as they tended to be in the shadows, and at the back of most 'events'.

We became quite good at hiding around street corners, me being 'protected' by the shields of my mates. The worst injuries were to legs, and my shins in particular (which my mates seemed to neglect when positioning a riot shield). At least the camera was protected. I used to get film for nothing, and shot frame after frame. During my time there, I probably shot a thousand rolls of film, each thirty-six frames, maybe only three thousand usable. All the film went straight to an RUC lab for processing, and I never saw any of the photographs. Any that were used later in identification could not be attributed to me, and neither could I claim copy-write or responsibility – but you wouldn't want to, would you (or is it me)?

Chapter 5

August 1968

Maureen Conlan lived in the Bogside area of 'Derry with her six children, and without her husband. He was in Parkhurst, serving 20 years for his part in a pub bombing in Hampshire. Maureen would describe herself as a mother, wife and committed supporter of 'the cause', and the IRA. Her children were indoctrinated too, and shared the hatred of the English, the Queen and Protestants generally.

Living next-door to the Conlans were the McBirney family, also with six children. She was also without a husband, who was in Compound 16 in the Maze Prison, and was going to be there for the foreseeable future for his part in an attack on an RUC Police Station; it had resulted in the death of two police officers, and four of his own hooded comrades. Both families had 15-year-old sons called Billy. Because he was six months older, Billy Conlan was known as Billy One, and Billy McBirney as Billy Two. It was the popular belief that both boys had the same father, although no one would have dared to suggest such a thing to Mrs Conlan.

It was a typical Saturday night; the kids were running riot, and Maureen was short on patience and long on Murphy's finest ale. As she left the pub, she heard the shouting, mayhem, gunshots, sirens and the intimidating (yeah right!), sound of batons on riot shields. The riot was in full swing as a protest about the earlier arrest of Bernadette Devlin, and general 'hard-line' tactics employed by the Military and RUC. It was, of course, fuelled by 'the drink', other reasons now largely forgotten.

She ventured closer, telling herself that she would go and see that the kids were ok in a minute, and, without intending to get involved, just poked her head around the corner. It was all happening. She sort of got carried along by the excitement of it all, and the mob hysteria – picked up a brick and got stuck in with the rest of them. It was good to be able to strike back at the bastards who had locked up her husband, and ruined her life. The foul-mouthed insults she hurled made her feel better, and some of her missiles struck the target.

She retreated to catch her breath, thought about the kids, and went home to check on them; she needed a wee anyway. Mavis, her eldest daughter, had sorted the kids out, and had everything under control. On impulse, she grabbed the jumble-sale box from behind the backdoor, and went back to the fun. There was a bit of a lull in proceedings, a bit of a stand-off with a line of troops facing a line of rioters, eyeballing each other whilst the local Priest tried to calm things down. She didn't quite know why she did it, certainly six pints helped, but she walked to the front of the rioters, stepped out into the rubble strewn 'no-mans land', put the box down in front of her: "Does yers want a cuppa tea boys?", and, without waiting for a reply… "Well here's the fuckin cups!" and proceeded to throw the contents of the box at the troops.

It would have been funny if her arm hadn't been as strong, and her aim so good. It was, however, a really good photo opportunity, isolated from the crowd, well-lit and without motion at times. 'They should be good sharp images', I thought, as the riot continued.

Me, and my two mates were crouched in a shop doorway, and we were joined by a Snatch Squad of four. Their role was to grab any of the rioters that they could, and drag them to the rear of the troops, and hand them over to the RUC. The troops had been subjected to hours of missiles, and abuse; they were getting more and more frustrated by their inability to respond. Their instructions were to not retaliate (not to chuck stuff back), not to shoot anyone; they were the coconuts at the Bogside fairground coconut shy.

The troops moved slowly back, drawing the bravest, and most active, rioters forward until level with our doorway. The Snatch Squad ran out, grabbed two of the stone throwers, which coincided with the troops rushing forward, causing the main body of rioters to run away again leaving the captured two isolated. Dragging them through the middle of the assembled troops to be arrested was the objective. The frustration got the better of the troops, and the 'prisoners' were battered, bleeding and concussed upon arrival at the rear, apparently having tripped over the rubble that they had thrown, and bumped their heads on soldiers' truncheons.

The confrontation with the rioters had started on Saturday evening, and continued unabated, until five o'clock on Monday morning. Most of us were there for the duration. Troop injuries were not reported.

On Monday evening, Billy One heard the banging on the door, and was first down the stairs with Maureen behind him, shrieking at him: "Stay away from the door, Billy!" Mavis had spread her arms at the top of the stairs, holding back the other pyjama clad four.

Ignoring his mother's warning, Billy got to the door as it burst inwards from the force of a six-foot copper's shoulder. That, combined with the closing speed of Billy rushing to the door as it opened, made the consequences inevitable. Billy crumpled, legs gone, head back, now going in the opposite direction. Maureen stopped momentarily, glanced at the bloody mess that used to be her beloved son's smiling face, and threw herself at the incoming RUC men.

Chapter 6

August 1968

Dan 'Shamus' Carroll had been a committed career RUC officer for 20 years, and really had 'seen it all'. That was until he met Maureen Conlan. He was a veteran of many a bar fight, street brawl, even police station punch-ups between colleagues. Maureen was something else; she was possessed, demonic – a whirlwind of flying fists, elbows, feet, teeth and spit. His bulk filled the doorway, and because of it, he took the brunt of the attack.

To right of the door was a pool cue, left there waiting for her husband to fulfil his parting promise to Billy to play pool in the club with him on the night of his return.

In the tight confines of the hallway, Maureen managed to stun Dan momentarily with the venom of her attack. This gave her time to grab the pool cue, and then it was lights-out for Dan. He fell forwards, and to the right, sliding down the door, landing on the unconscious Billy. That gave room for the second wave, but he was no match for Maureen's potting skills either, and went down without much trouble. It then became a little confused and (convenient for some), no one seems to remember whose gun Maureen grabbed... but the recovering Dan was convinced that he only shot her in the side of the head because he was protecting his colleagues from certain death at the hand of this, now armed, mad woman. The bone splinters, blood, and what had previously been contained in Maureen's skull were splattered all over the wall, carpet, and the still standing RUC officers.

The explosion of the gunshot and the gas pressure in such a confined area was deafening, and as the ringing in the ears of everyone subsided into stunned silence, Billy began to take in the scene: the sobbing from up-stairs, the smoke beginning to drift upwards. His eyes flicked between Dan, the gun in his hand, his mother without a face (and strangely without a gun), the abstract art feature wall, the group hug at the top of the stairs – and back to the eyes of the man who had just killed his mother…and the light fading from the eyes of his Mammy.

Chapter 7

October 1968

After a few weeks of dashing from riot to riot in 'Derry, it was 'suggested' that I should attend a training course in Hereford, where I would learn survival techniques, concealment, and avoidance training.

My mentor in Hereford was Phil, a quietly spoken Yorkshire lad about my age, smaller than me, but solid muscle. His neck was the size of my leg. I was tremendously impressed by him, and knew instantly that I could trust him to get me through the course. It was a hard time, with a lot of uncomfortable days and nights in the freezing cold, driving rain and mist that is normal for October in the Brecon Beacons. We formed a strong bond, and shared many experiences that are only understandable if you have been pushed to the limits of endurance. The experience certainly shaped my life, and I have never lost the stamina that it developed. My level of fitness has gone up and down over the years (mainly down now), but the stamina has always stayed.

Phil and I lived together, ate, drank, climbed, hid, ran and slept together (only for warmth) it's surprising what you do when you have to. I can remember being roped together on a rock wall in Wales, having been climbing since dawn, when Phil announced that he needed a crap. You certainly get to know someone when you are tied together, helping your mate drop his trousers, guiding him so that he craps into the cling film that you can then wrap the deposit in, and use to keep your hands warm for a few minutes.

It was at Hereford that I first met Mike O'Brian. There were a lot of Mikes about, so he became 'OB'. He was doing the full course (along with everyone else, other than me), so he, and everyone else, looked down on me as being a lesser mortal in the world of the supermen that I had been thrust into. We didn't get on too well, in fact, we didn't get on at all – but that changed when our paths crossed again in the January. I guess, at that time, anyone who gains admission to the Regiment is focused on that alone; they have to be to do what they do, and survive. I later became very appreciative of his training, skills and intuitive survival abilities. He had an almost sixth sense that gave him an uncanny way of knowing what was coming next.

I had a week at home after Hereford, and spent Christmas trying to get back to normality, but failed miserably. The testosterone, stress, physical exertion and tension of 'Derry and Hereford takes its toll, and Christmas was a blur of sullen dark moods, interspersed with hyper activity, outrageous drunken, rude behaviour, all excused and explained by mother, bless her, as: "He's been through such a lot 'over there,' you know."

New Year came, and I got back to 'Derry, and into the old routine within hours. It was a busy weekend, with gangs kicking off in several places at once, and we dashed from hot-spot to hot-spot, backing up hard-pressed patrols. You might think that the rioters were mainly young men, but in truth, a rioting crowd was a mix of old and young, girls and boys, men and women. There was usually an element of alcohol involved, which fuelled the aggression and bravado. Limited as the troops were by 'rules of engagement', in the main, they stood their ground, and took what was thrown at them – literally. So, we dashed back and forth through The Diamond (the square in the middle of the city), to Butchers Gate. There, with my camera, I was, again, the target for the abuse, which had become normal in a riot situation. They knew what I was there for, and I was beginning to be recognised – a familiar figure. We suffered the normal, abusive insults, references to parentage, the Queen and anything else they could think of.

Their 'focus' (pun intended), was on the spectacle-wearing cameraman with the big lens; this is when I was first given the name 'Speccy Five Eyes'.

Chapter 8

January 1969

I was whisked into Crossmaglen (known as XMG), the fortified Army Base that was in the middle of South Armagh's 'bandit country'. I was introduced to OB, as if he was a stranger, and we shook hands without acknowledging any 'history'. It was made clear that what we were about to be asked had a 'no thanks' option, but it was also clear that a lot of time and effort (for effort – read money), had been put into training. I didn't hesitate for a second: see mother, not brave – just bloody stupid.

After kitting out, and a good nosh-up, we flew out of XMG that evening in two helicopters, a total patrol of 12. We were to 'observe' one of many, very isolated border crossings that were used to smuggle anything from North to South, like condoms, and South to North like fags, petrol and PE (plastic explosive). Fashionable at the time was C4 or Semtex, and we had intelligence that a consignment was due to be shipped that night, at that crossing. As the RUC wanted photos, OB and I were in the lead group, and we settled into the hedgerow overlooking the crossing point with 10 camouflaged, and blacked-up silent figures to the left and right of us. It was eerily silent. I couldn't see or hear any of the guys we were with; they had melted into the ground.

The peace was short lived; we had walked into (crept actually), a trap and started to take some serious fire from several points either side, and to the front of us. It was short lasting, but intense, and I pushed myself as deep into the ground as I could to make as small a target as possible. OB had dived almost on top of me, and wasn't moving. I wriggled out from under him, and saw that he had blood running down his face from some injury to his head.

The crack of the rounds going into the ground, trees and undergrowth was terrifying; it's not as loud as you might think, and you don't hear the bang of a gun like in a film – it's just not like that.

OB still wasn't moving; I grabbed him by the collar, and began to drag him into better cover. He was surprisingly easy to move on the wet slippery grass, and we covered about five metres when, as quickly as it started, it stopped. Silence fell; troops began to whisper, take stock and see what the damage was. A distant engine rumble signified the departure of the bandits, back South from where they had come. I think we were quite relieved that we had been instructed not to pursue South, only North.

There were three minor casualties, including a miraculous deflected round that had just clipped OB's helmet, and grazed the side of his head just above his right ear – another inch would have done it. He 'came-to' when it was all over, and had to have it all explained to him. Despite his protests, he was in sickbay overnight whilst the rest of us got hammered in the bar.

The stories of near misses and bravery were grossly exaggerated, and no doubt embellished, to include hundreds of people who were not there. It's a strange fact that 'war stories' are usually untrue; the true ones rarely or never get told, so this might just be the exception.

One of the stories that got embellished (but not by me), was the story told to OB about how I had dragged him half a mile under constant fire from heavy machine guns etc, etc, and saved his life. In later moments of drunken sentimentality, with arms draped around each other (only for support you understand), he would profess everlasting love, debt and gratitude.

Oh, how we laughed.

Chapter 9

February 1969

Back in 'Derry again, it seemed quite tame, and, I must admit, there was an element of bravado, and a bit of a swagger about me that I seemed to have developed. I was still fairly quiet, and a bit of a loner back in the Unit, but had gained a certain credibility that was new to me. I occasionally picked up a half sentence as I passed a group who would say things like 'that's him' and 'he's the one who...'

Then back to XMG, and OB and I boarded a Lynx helicopter for a romantic weekend away together – a drop site four kilometres from a remote farm that we were going to watch. It was known that an IRA Unit had dropped some weapons into the farm for safe-keeping some weeks earlier, and we had strong intelligence that suggested they were about to be recovered and used. Our role was to photograph any of the visitors so that the RUC could identify them at a later date.

We had several options that had code words that OB could radio in, to either be extracted or to get the cavalry in. This was his decision, and if he thought the circumstances were right potentially, we could clear the lot out in one hit, the hardware (arms), the IRA Unit and the naughty farmer who was baby-sitting.

It was dark, cold, wet and miserable and we lay in the grass waiting for the quiet to return, as the Lynx banked away. and dipped over the small hill behind us. I was about ready to move, had begun to get my night vision, and everything was quiet. OB signalled to me to wait, and for another 5 minutes, the silence surrounded us like an inaudible fog. There was nothing to indicate anyone was around, but still he waited… and then I saw it. Some distance away, maybe even half a kilometre, hard to tell in the dark – but the unmistakable fag glowing as the smoker turned to face us whilst having a drag.

He was at the top of a hill on the lane ahead of us, which ultimately would lead to the main road between Omagh and Strabane. I have no idea how OB knew he was there, but he did. In whispered instructions he told me the plan, and we set off, silently, to the fag we had seen.

Although in the opposite direction to our target farm, OB wanted to have a chat, and make sure we were in the clear. The fag end got closer, but would disappear, heading back down the other side of the hill for a while, only to then reappear. The fag was clearly pacing about, but quite openly, not fearing for his life, as he should have been.

"Jesus an' Mary! Where the fuck did you come from? You scared the shit out of me". Looking down the pointy end of an SA80 assault rifle has a real focusing effect, and there was no hesitation, and no doubting the truth of his answers.

"What're you doing up here at this time of night?"

"I'm waitin' fer me mate to finish, then it's my go", he said, with a nod towards the car just visible parked on the verge, a couple of hundred meters back towards the main road.

"Your go at what?", OB asked.

"We brought a girl with us in the car wen the pub shut, and she's up for doin' us both. I've got a sloppy 'two's up'."

"It's not your lucky night feller, get in your car and fuck off out of here. NOW!"

Thirty seconds later, the car set off back the way it had come, the sound fading into the distance.

"Has that blown it, OB?"

"No, he won't connect us to anything. But he won't get it blown tonight though." OB laughed at his own joke, and we turned to retrace our route, and then on another five K's towards the border with Southern Ireland.

It took three hours of careful walking, keeping in the shadows, constantly alert, my eyes fixed on OB's Burgan backpack.

Chapter 10

February 1969

It was about an hour before dawn, and we settled into our ditch under a thick hedge. Behind us was a reasonably dense wood, through which we had crept to emerge on a hill overlooking the farmhouse, barns and outbuildings. OB had navigated well to get us to this exact position in total darkness.

"Get yer head down, mate, nothing is going to happen until daybreak." Over the years in the army, I had learned to sleep and eat at every opportunity – you never knew when the next chance would be. Within minutes, I was asleep, with OB crouched beside me, constantly looking and listening for any sounds of life. I woke at around 6 o'clock, mainly because of the cold. We shared chocolate bars, and hard-tack (biscuits) and watched the farm slowly coming to life.

Everything looked different, now, in misty daylight, and I was surprised just how close we were to the buildings. The field ahead was about 100 yards wide at this point, with a stout wooden fence on its boundary, with a lane running left to right next to the open farmyard. The farmhouse was set back slightly on the left edge, the barn opposite on the right with outbuildings in the middle, two cars parked between. I would certainly be able to photograph people from our position, and we were very well hidden from view.

Two figures left the farmhouse, got into one of the cars and left the farm. A third figure appeared at the farmhouse door, stretched, yawned, and shuffled wearily across to the barn. He pulled open double doors, pushing them both outwards with a foot. They swung slowly until grounding, almost at maximum opening distance, and the man went inside. We heard the sound of a reluctant engine starting, coughing, spluttering, and finally bursting into life with a roar that then settled into a rather lumpy tick-over.

Clouds of smoke and fumes began to emerge from the barn, and the engine note changed as the vehicle was manoeuvred inside the barn. An old and battered tractor slowly emerged from the barn with a large horse box trailer pulled behind it. It swayed, and trundled across the uneven yard to stop at the entrance. The driver climbed down, and walked across the lane to the gate into the field ahead of us, and opened it.

I looked questioningly at OB, who shook his head reassuringly. We didn't need to speak; he instinctively knew my question. My heart was pounding; this wasn't what I had expected. Gate now wide open, the man climbed back onto the tractor and drove into the field. The sound of the tractor slowly increased, drowning out the sound of the jackdaw's early morning calls. He drove to the left of us, and then turned, so that he was parallel to the ditch we were in, about ten yards in front of us, and kept coming towards us.

The tractor was grey, streaked with red rust, brown mud (and worse), chunky tyres throwing clods of earth into the air behind it. It spluttered and coughed across the field through the early morning mist, rocking from side to side, like a ship in a rough sea of grass. It continued towards us, getting closer, chugging alongside the ditch, and then stopped. The driver climbed down, and disappeared from view behind the trailer. We waited. I realised that I had not breathed for a while, and tried to calm my heart rate. I could smell the oil from the tractor, and even feel the heat from it as it continued to chug, splutter, cough and tick-over in front of us.

Chapter 11

February 1969

I was rigid, frozen stiff, when I felt the cold, hard, metallic 'thing' in the back of my neck.

"Good mornin'!" I looked right without moving my head, and saw the end of another SLR firmly pressed against OB's neck.

"Why don't we have us a little walk down the field, and have a little chat." Painful push in the back of my neck, and I started to stand. We had heard nothing; the tractor engine noise had masked everything, and we were well and truly screwed. OB stood too, and we extricated ourselves from the ditch and stood, exposed, in the morning sunshine at the edge of the field. Another prod in the back of the neck encouraged me to step forward towards the horse box trailer.

My 9mm Browning was removed from the holster on my belt, and OB's SA80 was unceremoniously snatched from his grasp. A savage blow from the butt of an SLR sent OB sprawling.

"Not so fuckin clever now, are yers?" Perhaps, I too, was a bit slow in obeying, and before I could apologise, was rewarded with a spectacular firework display of vivid colours, and fell face down in the field.

I don't remember the kicking, the abuse, the passing of time, or the journey in the horse box. I hurt everywhere.

I tentatively opened my eyes, but only one worked. We were in what appeared to be a pig-sty, concrete floor with a scattering of straw, square room, corrugated roof. There was a stable door in the middle of the wall, two floor-to-roof steel girders set into the concrete floor, to which OB and I were secured with plastic cable ties – cheap, effective and impossible to break. I tentatively explored the inside of my mouth; a new gap at the front, and someone else's lips. My right arm was throbbing somewhere around the elbow, and it hurt like hell if I tried to pull against the cable ties. I looked at OB, who was franticly rubbing the cable tie restraints up and down on the girder behind his hands.

"You ok?", was what I tried to say, but it came out as some foreign language that neither of us understood.

He looked across at me and said: "Play dead for a while, mate, an' I'll sort it. Sorry I got us into this, but I'll sort it, promise."

He looked a mess, as I probably did. He had a lot of dried blood around his nose and mouth and looked, well, different. In the circumstances, it was a bit bizarre to think of these things, but he looked a bit like a hamster, and, perhaps because of shock, stress, fear or whatever, I began to laugh. That caused a new sensation, and possibly because of fear, I couldn't stop my bladder function and pissed myself. The warmth spread along my stomach and thighs, and, I must admit was quite pleasant for a few minutes, but soon turned to cold discomfort.

The door burst open, and I was confronted by a silhouetted figure against the light from the door behind him who brandished OB's SA80 in our general direction, throwing a casual, "They're back with us", over his shoulder to some unseen confederate.

Kicking my legs to one side he stood between us. "You bastards fucked up a good shag last night." He stooped to inspect my securing cable ties – which is where he died.

OB, silently, like a ghost, encircled his neck with one arm, locked his other into his hand, twisted both with a jerk and broke his neck. The whole thing took seconds; he caught his SA80 before it hit the ground, turned, and, in one fluid movement, hit the incoming 'confederate' just above the bridge of the nose with the short barrel. His nose exploded, and he sank to the floor, oblivious, probably never to get up again, but I didn't look at him again to find out how he was.

OB did the pocket thing with them, and came up with a rusty, but sharp, pocketknife; he cut my cable ties and helped me to stand. It was at this point that I realised how painful my right arm was, and yelped as he grabbed it to pull me up. He stripped the belt off the prostrate 'nose-job', and used it to secure my arm to my side, and we stood either side of the door and listened.

Hens were clucking somewhere, and a dog barked in the distance, otherwise it was quiet. With a flat hand towards me, he indicated that I was to stay put, and he eased himself cautiously out of the door and disappeared. I felt sick, dizzy, and was near to throwing up, but had nothing substantial in my gut to get rid of. My face hurt like hell, my lips were twice their normal size, I could taste blood, newfound gaps in my teeth, and my arm was useless, probably broken.

Bizarrely, I was concerned that anyone who saw me might notice that I had pissed myself, and wondered how I could cover up the wetness on my combats.

Chapter 12

February 1969

He was away for what seemed like a long time, but was probably only a few minutes. I was cold, wet and shivering, and I guess was in danger of going into shock.

"It's clear, come on, old mate, let's have a brew; the lads are on their way. Chummy left my radio on the kitchen table – looks like it's been on for a while, and the battery's about done. They were on the wrong channel, and have probably been skipping about to see what they could pick up. The other car we saw has gone, and, apart from those two, there's only an old guy in the farmhouse, but he's in a wheelchair, so isn't going anywhere. I seem to have tripped over the phone", he said with a smile, "and the wires seem to have come out of the wall." With an arm under my left shoulder, we shuffled across the yard and through the open door.

"He", (nodding towards the farmer, if that is who he was), "Isn't too bright, but he probably knows more that he's letting on." The kitchen was warm – the smell of a wood burner, stone floor, windows front and back with a room beyond the stairs. "Sit there, mate, and keep an eye on the lane."

OB wasn't kidding about the wheelchair not moving; it was trapped against the wall by a bookcase that OB had up-ended. The fact that the guy had no legs was a bit of a clue to OB's confidence in him staying put. My camera was on the kitchen table, covered in mud, but otherwise seemed ok. I was presented with a brown-stained, chipped mug, accompanied by a grin and a wink.

"Sorry mate, milk smells a bit iffy, so it's black – but four sugars though, ok? Right, I'm off to check on our two friends out there, and have a poke about. Keep an eye on the lane, and Old MacDonald here." Thrusting my Browning butt first at me, he left.

Old Mac and I exchanged glances, and I moved slightly, so that I had a better view of the lane beyond the barn and out across the fields. The tea was foul, but hot and sweet, and I managed to juggle it, and the Browning, with my left hand without spilling any tea or shooting myself in the foot. Old Mac was saying nothing, just looked surly, unhappy and defeated. He was in his seventies, I guessed, not well groomed, in fact, a scruffy bugger. He was not looking confident, and his eyes flicked about the room, clearly wondering what was in store for him. He had, of course, been party to OB's radio coms, so he knew that the RUC would soon be all over him like a rash.

OB returned: "Both goners, them two, I'm afraid – not!"

Turning to Old MacDonald: "Right, old mate, you and me are going to play a game." Dragging the bookcase away to make room for the wheelchair, he moved Old Mac into the middle of the room.

"Now, do you remember how it goes? I look for somethin' you've hidden, an', as I get closer, you say 'warmer', and if I go the other way, you say 'colder'. Get it? Yeah! Course you do. Now, this time, I'm changing the rules a bit. Unless I get to find it, it's you that gets warmer, 'cos I've got a kettle full of boiling water. Get the idea? Right then, shall I start in here."

Without hesitation, he began: "Loose floorboards, under the settee, in there." Old Mac gestured towards the other room with a nod.

"Good lad", OB said, "That's saved a lot of kettle boiling." It was probably the stress and tension of the situation, but I just could not stop laughing. It was such a funny moment, but I guess you had to be there.

OB carried four British Army SLRs into the kitchen, and dumped them on the table. He then reappeared with two ammunition boxes, which he dropped on the floor, and two pistols, which he stuffed into his belt, and pulled his camouflage jacket down over them, and went back into the other room. Two more SLRs, two US Army Armolite, AR10s, and a Russian AK47 followed. Although I didn't realise it then, all of these took the same 7.62mm ammunition, which I thought was quite clever of our Irish friends.

"Bingo! That's what we came for. Shame we couldn't get the rest of the boys who were coming to collect them, eh, Sam?"

I had been distracted, and had not seen the two RUC Land Rovers until they were almost at the farm entrance, but the sound of their engines was drowned by the rotor noise of two Wessex choppers. The cavalry had arrived. There was a flurry of activity, a brief Sitrep (Situation Report), and an update given on the move by OB. I was attacked by a Medic who slapped a needle straight through my trouser leg.

I went to sleep holding another man's hand, but don't tell anyone.

Chapter 13

March 1969

I was struggling to open my eyes; it felt like my lids had been glued together. My mouth was like the inside of a prop forward's jock strap.

I lay still, and tried to identify the slight noise I could hear, a sort of rustling. With a supreme effort, I managed to get one eye at a time open, and then wait, whilst they both drifted about in different directions, finally coming into focus. She was bending over me, straightening sheets and generally fussing about. She was all white starch, enormous blue eyes and the top of an intriguing cleavage.

"Where am I?"

"Oh! Hello, nice of you to join us. You are in Altnagelvin Hospital in 'Derry. You came in yesterday afternoon with, amongst other things, a broken arm." Sod the arm, I thought, I'm in love. "We've had a bit of an operation to put it right, and it will be in that (gestures towards the plaster cast that I hadn't noticed) for a wee while, I'm afraid."

"But it's my right arm; how am I going to manage everything, you know, eat and stuff? I do such a lot with my right arm?" She stopped, broke into a huge smile that matched mine.

"Ach! It's the devil in yer, to be sure it is." ...and she was gone. A succession of people came and went, told me what to do and what not to do, all of which went into the 'I know better' box for disposal. My CO came, and told me what had cracked off, and that I was being shipped back to Devizes to recover and to await my demob, which was due at the end of the year. I asked about OB, and was told that he was 'out of the country', but he knew what was happening to me, sent his best wishes.

And that was that.

Goodbye, Ireland (possibly, maybe, perhaps).

Chapter 14

September 1971

The injustice of the inquest outraged him, and Billy knew that, one day, he would avenge his mother's death, for Daddy, for his sisters and for himself. He played the scene over and over in his head: how he would look into those eyes again, and how he would see the light go out in those eyes as the bullet entered his head. He dreamt it; he saw it in the rain puddle; he could see it in the shadows as he walked the streets; he could smell it and taste it; he lived it. He would take his revenge upon everyone that played a part in the killing of Mammy, even if it took years, even if it cost him his life, too.

He made notes at the inquest; he recorded names (except those of the soldiers who were behind screens), dates, places, statements, the lies and the truths. It had taken a year for the inquest to be heard, and he had known what the outcome would be. He knew that it would exonerate everyone. No one would be brought to justice, and no one would be punished, unless he did it himself. But that was ok; he would do it, he could do it, he just needed a bit if help, and he knew where to get it.

The local IRA men were idiots, they would not be able to help him, but he knew that they knew the people who could. He set about cultivating them, doing errands, delivering packages, and passing messages that made no sense to him. Now 16, having grown up fast, and with more life experience than many his age, he was finally holding a gun, passed through the fence after being used in an attack on a RUC patrol. It was still warm, and had the distinctive smell of the propellant and hot oil. He was to wrap it, conceal it and deliver it to the Westland Street Betting Shop two hours after the 'event'.

He was trusted, accepted, and was considered to be a potential career soldier in the IRA of the future. The betting shop was closed and in darkness – door unlocked and empty, but for the figure behind the counter, protected by a security grill. No words were exchanged, as he slid the parcel across the counter, through the opening in the security screen into the hands of Aedan Carney. Billy turned to leave, and then stopped. Aedan was the IRA Commander who could give him what he wanted. This was the opportunity he had worked towards. "Can we talk?", Billy asked, tentatively.

"About what, fella?"

"About my Mammy, and the proddy bastards that killed her." There was silence for a long moment whilst Aedan considered how to respond.

"Not now, and not here. I'll be in the back bar in the Bogside (Inn), in an hour."

The Bogside Bar was thick with smoke, noise and bodies, three deep at the bar, beer was spilt, sticky floor, the sort of place that makes you wipe your feet when you leave. Billy cautiously 'sideways walked' and swerved, turning left and right avoiding the head height pints of Murphy's that crossed his path, and made his way to the rear bar of the pub. Here it was quieter, but still busy.

Aedan sat at a small table, full of glasses, some empty, and some full, with an overflowing ashtray. He was in deep conversation with a man Billy vaguely recognised. Aedan glanced up, said a word to his friend who turned, glanced at Billy, stood and taking his pint with him, drifted away. Aedan hooked a foot around the leg of a stool, and dragged it to the table, nodding at Billy and then at the stool. Billy sat, took at deep breath and said: "I need a gun; I've a job to do." Aeden laughed, a deep belly laugh that made his considerable belly wobble, and caused several in the room to look in their direction. Leaning closer, Billy, with passion and venom said; "I mean it, Mr Carney. I want to get the people that did fer me mammy."

"S'not that simple laddie, I give you a gun and the first thing you'll do is miss the fuckin barn door you're aiming at. The second thing you'll do is shoot yourself in the fuckin foot."

Billy sat back, a little deflated, and at a bit of a loss as to how to convince Aeden of his determination. Billy took another deep breath, and trying to suppress the anger he could feel welling up – he didn't like being laughed at – he carried on; "I need your help to teach me too, Mr Carney."

Billy knew that Aedan could give him what he wanted, the gun, the ammunition, the training, the information about movements, the transport and the escape route – there it all was. He knew he couldn't do it tomorrow. Another pause, and the smile went from Aeden's face and he continued.

"Here's what I'll do Billy. I'll get you in touch with the right people, and we'll see if we can teach you what you need to know, but I can tell you laddie, that it won't be easy for you, and there will be a price to pay." He smiled again.

Not all was done in that conversation, but in the weeks and conversations that followed, it was. There was, as he had warned Billy, a price to pay, but he was willing to agree to all their conditions. The price was, effectively, the end of his life in exchange for the end of several others. A lifetime serving 'the cause', to undertake whatever was asked of him in the name of 'the cause', never to question, always to follow orders – no matter what.

Some weeks after this initial conversation, Billy met his mentor for the next six months, and his host, at a South Armagh pig farm. Joe 'The Tank' Murphy was an IRA Commander with a fearsome reputation. Joe was a big lad, who commanded respect because of his size, if nothing else. The enjoyment he derived from the removal of kneecaps, and the brutal beatings he dished out certainly enhanced his reputation. Billy owed much of his success in achieving his revenge objectives to the guidance he received from Joe.

In the months that followed, he worked hard on the farm to "Gott'a 'ern yer keep Boy", as Joe had put it. The hours were long – up at dawn, working late into the afternoon, before then 'going to school'. School to Billy was the route to his goal. He spent many hours shooting cans and fag packets, and even more hours studying schedules, movements and road maps.

The test came in the summer of 1972.

In the back of the van, he was on his way to a nondescript terraced house on the Ballymurphy estate,

Belfast. "Yer goin to do a six pack, Billy. Do this right an we'll see yer get what yer want." Tank Murphy had said. Billy knew this was the reality of it; his quest depended upon it – the only way that he was going to be able do what he really wanted to do. These were merely obstacles to his objective that he had to overcome, not real people that needed to be considered or sympathised with; they were, after all, only people that had done wrong. They deserved what they got. He was scared, yes, but excited too; this was his chance to prove that he was ready, capable of inflicting pain and, yes, death, if that's what it took.

His role was to enter behind the other four men, and as they parked in the dark, wet evening, Joe passed him the gun. It was a silenced Welrod, originally designed for veterinary use, but ideal for this purpose. He had used it before in the woods behind Joe's farm, and knew what it would do at close range, useless though, at anything over ten feet. Billy was not intending to be more than inches away when he used it.

Gary Donaghan, rightly or wrongly, had been convicted in the eyes of the Belfast paramilitaries of dealing in drugs, without approval and, more importantly, without paying taxes into the coffers of the local controlling IRA Unit. There could only be one sanction. To protect the authority of the unit, they had sought the help of 'Tank's' Armagh unit; they needed to re-establish authority.

Gary was peeling potatoes, carrots and onions in the kitchen when they came through the kitchen door. There was no drama – not a sledge hammer through the glass, not a burst through the door or window; they just walked in, as if invited. Two into the living room to terrorise and intimidate his family, leaving three in the kitchen, two to hold his arms and pin him to the worktop, facing the hob and the extractor fan. Billy first shot through his elbows, then his knees, and, finally, his ankles. It was easier this way, starting from the top, as Joe had advised. Starting with ankles would have meant that it would have been harder to keep Gary standing. As it was, Gary was clinging to the cutlery drawer, holding his breath, and hoping that not breathing in or out would minimise the pain – it didn't.

Chapter 15

April 1973

Billy knew that it would be difficult; Joe had warned him that this was different from kneecapping – not a can or fag packet that didn't cry out, or bleed and potentially fight back – this was flesh and blood. He was focussed, determined, and knew that what he was doing was right: he was putting to rights the wrongs that had been done to him, his sisters, mammy and daddy. He was starting with Dan Carroll.

The garden gate was open, and he walked down the path, turned right at the front door, and walked around the corner to the back door of the modest semi-detached house.

Dan had bought the house in Ballymoney with Mary 15 years ago, and now, almost mortgage free, he could start to think about a holiday, perhaps a caravan. As he drove home, he thought about next year, without the £40 mortgage payment each month he could get a new car, if he could persuade Mary that she didn't really need a new kitchen and bathroom. To be fair, the dog will bugger up the kitchen, and Helen (14), will spend her life in the bathroom, 'so what's in it for us, Mary?', he mentally asked her.

It hadn't been too bad a day really, two little shits locked up for the night for doing an off-licence, and some progress on ID'ing the stunning blonde with big tits. It was inconsiderate of her to be dead when we found her, and we couldn't understand why her nipples were so hard and prominent. Is that some sort of rigor mortis effect, he wondered? We've got a really good lead on where the petrol tanks are that are being used to store the stuff coming over the border – I need to get onto that in the morning. That would mean a fair drive out to Castlederg...but, if he got the timing right, it could mean lunch in his favourite pub in Douglas Bridge

It was good that things had quietened down in terms of 'the troubles'; it was always there though, under the surface. He still checked his car every morning, but he had taken to leaving his issued revolver at the station; he was not comfortable taking it home. It seemed sort of inconsiderate and disrespectful to do that, and involve his family in all the shit that being in the RUC brought with it. He thought about ringing Andy, and asking him if he fancied a pint, but then his dinner would be ready, Mary would be at the door, dog to walk: 'Argh, what the hell'.

He parked in the drive; it was beginning to rain, and was getting slightly misty as the colder air descended. Lights were being turned on, as neighbours settled in for an evening in front of the television. He got out, and stopped momentarily to look at the strange car parked on the other side of the road. It was strange as in 'not normally parked there' as opposed to 'unusual'. That said, it was a good-looking car. Only an Escort, but it had all the trimmings, big wheel arches, fat tyres, four spot-lights and some lettering down the side. He was still thinking about it, as he turned and walked to the back door.

"Hi, love!" As he flung the back door wide, waiting for the Labrador assault that didn't happen.

It was wrong; there was the smell of food, faintly the sound of Helen's music (if that's what it's called), from upstairs; normality, but it just didn't quite feel right. With a puzzled frown, he opened the door to the living room, and slowly, began to take in the scene. He was calm, shocked – yes, but controlled, and a little removed from the reality. It didn't register with him in totality; he was transfixed, mouth open, the moment frozen in time.

"Do you remember me, Mr Carroll?"

Mary was sitting on the floor in the corner of the room, back to the wall with tape over her mouth and ankles, with her arms behind her, which he assumed were tied. He could see the tears, distress and fear that she couldn't communicate. Helen, immobile, blood pooling on the carpet. She was laying half on the settee and half on the floor head down, legs up, exposing her knickers. Dan was momentarily concerned about her modesty, and then focused upon the more serious implications of the situation.

"Yes! I remember you, Billy"

Dan began to take in the rest of the scene; Labrador 'Higgins', was lying in an unusual position by the window, head on one side with a lot of blood around his head. The table lamp was now an unlit floor lamp, and the coffee table was on its side and had spilt its magazine contents at Helen's feet (head actually).

"I'm here to put right the wrongs, Mr Carroll... (pause), you killed my mammy ...(pause), you know you did... (pause), you killed my family (no pause), you killed everything we had!" With increased volume and passion, he shouted: "You killed everything I had in our family."

Billy's outpouring subsided into sobs, and Dan wanted to comfort him; he really felt for the lad, but he knew that no sympathy, reasoning or logic would help resolve the situation that he and his family were in. The gun in Billy's hand wavered around the room, at Mary, then at him, then back to Mary. Occasionally, the floor was the target, and Dan tried to calculate the chances of getting across the room in the time it would take Billy to move his aim from Shag-pile to Sternum. It wasn't a gun he recognised; he assumed it was an IRA bargain, and wondered about its reliability, would it missfire, would it be off-target, would it jam? Probably not, and he was not going to gamble. Be cool, remember the training, talk to him. Get him to talk.

Although Dan didn't recognise it, the gun was a prototype Berretta 93, nine mm, fresh off a fishing boat from Libya via Clogga Strand, a route that would be important to Billy in the next few hours.

"I watched my mammy die when you shot her, my sisters watched my mammy die when you shot her, for no reason. She didn't have a gun. She was no threat to you. You shot her because you could. Have you any idea how that feels? No, you don't do you?" Without a pause, he swung the gun towards Mary and fired one shot; her face didn't change – just a hole appearing in the centre of the grey tape. Blood, brain, tissue and bone exploded from what was left of the back of Mary's skull. Dan leapt forward, he knew that it was a futile gesture, but, outraged by Billy's callous act, driven by anger, without a thought for his own survival, he launched himself over the arm of the settee (and Helen's legs), to grapple with, to unarm and disable (actually to kill the bastard), the demented Billy One. In mid-flight, Dan's assault ended abruptly – stopped by a 9mm projectile, which entered the top of his head, travelling all the way through his skull, before coming to rest at his collarbone. He was dead before he hit the coffee table.

It was suddenly quiet. Ticking clock, distant music from upstairs, smoke lazily spiralling towards the ceiling.

Now calm, Billy was surprised at how easy it had been, how powerful he felt for the first time in his life. He had avenged his mammy, dad, who had died of cancer in Parkhurst, and his sisters, who were fragmented in various care homes and foster homes. He did not have time to enjoy the achievement though; he had a car waiting, and another job to do. Stepping carefully over Dan's body, around Helen's head, he left, going back through the kitchen and out into the evening twilight.

Chapter 16

April 1973

He was shaking a little when he got to the car. It was raining, cold, misty, the smell of cigarette smoke around. He guessed Pete had been pacing around, smoking, and wondering if he was going to appear out of the mist or if, he, (Pete), would need to resort to plan B, and get the fuck out.

He took a deep breath, and tried to control his shaking; he did not want Pete to see that he was anything but in control of himself and the situation. Pete had obviously seen him approaching, leaning across, left- hand opening the passenger door and right-hand starting the engine at the same time. The car was moving before Billy had shut the door. Nothing was said; Billy sank into the bucket seat of the stolen Escort Twin Cam, and was pushed back by the acceleration. Pete knew the route, the plan, the schedule – and he knew it was tight.

After a mile or so (and less then a minute), he said: "Everythin' ok?"

"Yeah, like clockwork; just drive and let me recover."

Billy ejected the magazine from the '93, replaced the three expended rounds, and reinserted the 15 round magazine. Pete was impressed by the cold efficiency and calmness that Billy exuded. Although exceeding 60mph through country lanes, he was able to observe Billy, and was chilled by the calm demeanour of a young 'kid' who had (potentially) just killed an 'RUC Family'. He wanted to ask but... there was a series of tight bends and junctions coming that he needed to concentrate on. He had driven rally cars on this road many times and was chosen by The Tank because he was good – very good. If he'd had the money, and the car, he could have been amongst the best, up there with Billy Coleman and Bertie Fisher.

They had 28 miles to cover to get to Newtownstewart, and needed to achieve that in less than 20 minutes, the time that The Tank had estimated that they had to get to target number two, five minutes inside, achieve everything and then get over the border and cover another 50'odd miles to the boat at Sligo. In total 1 hour and 45 minutes to catch a boat.

The noise in the car didn't allow real conversation, and the miles passed in a noisy blur. Both were focused, Pete on the task in hand, Billy on the task ahead. Several times the Escort slid wide, as Pete pushed beyond the limit, flashing by stone walls, street furniture and solid scenery with the accompanying "music" of the twin DCOE 40 Webber carburettors, and the straining Lotus Twin Cam, rushing towards the likely scene of the accident. It didn't happen, Pete really was good, and they slowed to a crawl. With lights off, they approached the imposing detached house on the outskirts of the town to the right of the road surrounded by a high laurel hedge.

Nothing was said. Billy merely nodded to Pete as he got out. They had been over this many times before, rehearsed by the Tank, almost to the point that both Pete and Billy wanted to kill him too.

The car moved off, Pete turning round as planned, so that the exit was unimpeded and direct. It also meant that the passenger door of the car was now nearest to the entrance to the house. Billy stepped into the drive, turning immediately to the left to avoid the gravel and the crunch that it would make, announcing his approach. All Billy could hear was the metallic clicking sound of the cooling engine at the end of the drive. Lights were on in four ground floor windows, curtains drawn in two of them. One upper-floor window was lit, again, curtains open, but after all, this was a remote house, not over-looked – the nearest habitation was nearly half a mile away.

Christopher Blears-Thompson, QC was 58, and seriously considering retirement; fishing from his boat at his Portumna Forrest Park Lodge was becoming more and more appealing. His problem was the isolation and incarceration with his loving, and increasingly demanding, nagging wife that deterred him from taking the plunge. He had done his bit, serving first as a Solicitor, then Barrister, JP and latterly as a Coroner.

He was 'comfortable', thank you very much, and felt that he had actually earned a leisurely, peaceful retirement – if only he could calm Mrs BT down, so that they (he) could enjoy the peace and solitude that the lodge offered. This weekend his son, Chris Junior, was over for the weekend with the delightful Maddie, soon to be Mrs Chris Junior. He topped up his glass, took a deep breath and left the kitchen, walking into the dining room where the other family members were gathered.

"About time you appeared, CBT", Anita (Mrs BT) said, with a genuine smile, "We were about to start without you."

Chris Junior turned away from the garden view, smiled at his father, walked to the settee that Maddie was snuggled in the corner of, took her hand and looked down at her upturned face. There was a pause, the window exploded; Chris seemed to jump into the air a foot or so, fell forward across Maddie, who screamed as his face disappeared in a cloud of red mist – a small hole in the back of his head, a large hole in the front. Mrs BT stood, mouth open, and turned towards the hole where the window used to be, and was propelled backwards as three rapid fire shots first hit her chest, her neck, just below her chin, and then her lower abdomen, as she hit her husband at knee level. CBT's instinctive reaction was to try and catch his wife and cushion her fall to the floor. This meant he was leaning forward, arms under his wife's shoulders, covered in her blood, bodily fluid, brain matter and skull-bone chips, when the shape materialised at the empty widow frame. He stopped, mid stoop, wife in arms, and met the eyes of hate at the window. Maddie was gasping for breath, clearly in deep shock, Chris Junior was continuing to bleed profusely, even though his heart had stopped pumping.

Billy knocked the remaining glass from the frame with the pistol, and leaned through the window: "Hello Mr Coroner, Sir". He was oblivious to the glass splinters that nicked his hand, and then the back of his neck, as he leaned through the window into the elegant dining room. "If you know who I am, it means you know you made the wrong decision in protecting the RUC bastard who killed my mother. I'm here to put that right. I'm leaving someone in your family to suffer like I've suffered, and will always suffer. I just want you to know what they will have to live with, what you created, even when you have gone. If you don't know who I am – well, I don't have time to explain."

Christopher Blears-Thompson, QC, died from a bullet wound to the head. He did not feel the other four bullets, but Billy felt each one as it hit, and sank deep into the body of this man who had failed to bring to justice the man who had destroyed his family.

Billy calmly turned away, leaving the traumatised Maddie to stare in vacant horror at the window, and the gently fluttering curtains.

Chapter 17

April 1973

He woke with a start, heart pounding, sweating, and took a moment or two to remember where he was and the events of the last few hours. The car was warm, and he was reacting to the post-adrenaline rush, which was probably why he had fallen asleep. Pete was driving slower now, as they approached Sligo. They had a few minutes in hand; the pace had been good, traffic light, and they were bang on schedule.

They crossed the river bridge, turning right onto Ballast Quay Road, running along-side the river wall on the right, small factories, warehouses and workshops on the left. It was dark, wet, badly lit and almost deserted. Just the odd lay-about, dog and carrier bag meandering between buildings. They joined The Deepwater Quay Road and moved on to the Port of Sligo Harbour Entrance.

Two hundred yards beyond the gates, the 'Patricia Mary' rocked gently at her moorings, running lights on, engine burbling, figure at the helm, two in yellow oilskins on deck, stowing nets, coiling ropes and generally preparing to go fishing on the high tide.

Pete stopped in the shadow of the warehouse, killed the lights, and held out his hand without taking his eyes from screen and mirror. Billy shook his hand,

and, without a word between them, lifted his rucksack from the foot-well, got out, walked behind the car and crossed to the waiting boat. Pete turned the car and was gone before Billy reached the boat.

A crewman was off the boat now, and already untying the mooring lines. With an exchange of nods, Billy dropped his bag to the deck, and followed it with a short jump down to the steadying arm of the second crewman. Another nod from him clearly indicated that he was wanted 'on the bridge'. He flinched momentarily, as the other man landed on the deck with a thud behind him, and the boat began to rock and drift away from the quay. The engine note picked up from a throb to a roar, and they were underway.

Collecting his bag, he picked his way carefully around and over the nets, pots and plastic containers, up a short flight of steps and into the warmth of the bridge.

"I want you down there", said without introduction or greeting, just an incline of the head toward the open door. This was at the front (pointy end) of the boat. "It will take us an hour to get out, and then I'll give you a shout. Don't throw up over anything, you'll find a bucket down there and very little else. My job is to get you to where you're going, not to ensure your comfort". With another exchange of nods, Billy headed for the doorway. "Hang-on, I want the gun first", holding out a hand. Billy dropped the bag, removed the gun from his jacket, ejected the mag and handed over both.

"Do we not have a lecture about safety, life-jackets and all that bollocks, then?" Billy asked. The smile told him that his Guide, Captor, Steward, Captain, or whatever he was, was sort of human. Collecting his bag again, he went through the door, down four steps, under the sign that said "DUCK", into what he supposed was called a cabin. It was sparse, a table bolted to the floor (deck possibly), with benches on two sides also bolted down. There was a table top stove of sorts, a few pans, a newspaper, mugs, tins of food; he was slightly amused to see that two of them were tins of Pilchards – what, on a fishing boat?

This was new to him, and he sat on a bench, moving the bucket with a foot so that it was between his legs. The engine noise was quite loud, the boat was beginning to pitch a bit, and, coupled with engine fumes and the smell of diesel fuel, he realised that he would need the bucket sooner rather than ... the first bucket moment arrived.

The Atlantic was not a friendly environment to Billy; the engine roared and fell with the pitching motion. He longed for fresh-air, stability and an end to the retching. There was a rhythm to it now, the retching usually coinciding with the dropping sensation, the reduction in engine note and the banging headache. It went on and on for hours, well, about forty minutes actually, and then things began to quieten down.

He wondered if this was the process that everyone went through before they came out of the other end wearing their shiny, new, scaly sea legs.

The engine roar was gone; it was replaced by a slow thump from the big marine diesel. The pitching had lessened too, and was more side to side than pointy to blunt. Which way is starboard anyway? After bobbing about for ten minutes or so, the engine note picked up, and the movement changed, giving him the impression that the boat was being manoeuvred.

With a great effort, he stood, bucket at the ready. When he blinked, he could see bright lights, but he needed to test his balance. He was a bit unsteady, but found that if he rocked in the opposite direction to the boat's movements, he began to feel better. He took deep breaths, and tried to get back in control of his innards. The retching lessened.

The Captain's head appeared, and said: "Time for you to go."

On wobbly legs, he retrieved his rucksack and went from table, to wall, to doorway and climbed the four steps back to the world, hitting his head on the low doorframe (which did not have a 'DUCK' sign on the inside). The fresh air greeted him, and he sucked in great lung fulls to try and clear his head. Outside the wheelhouse and on deck, he was astounded to see the massive ship towering above the little fishing boat with lines over its side, attaching it. Grabbed by his jacket, and manhandled to the side, the crew tied a rope around him and turned him to face the massive ship wall above him.

"Wait!" As the two vessels drifted apart, and then back together again: "Now, Climb!", the voice shouted in his ear.

The rope went tight, biting into his back, chest and armpits; he was pushed from behind, pulled from above and momentarily suspended, before crashing against the side of the ship and coming into contact with the suspended rope ladder. Instinctively, he grabbed hold, was hit hard by breath taking icy, cold spray, and he half climbed and was half dragged up the ladder.

I didn't say goodbye, he thought.

Chapter 18

April 1973

The Pentra was built in 1971 by Kristiansands Mekaniske Verksted AS, a Norwegian ship building company. She had had an 'interesting' life, several names, and several owners, and was currently registered in Liberia to a shipping company based in Nassau, Bahamas. She was 26,486 tonnes, and carried general cargo and containers from Africa, the Mediterranean and Black Sea ports into Europe and back. She was crewed by six Indonesians, a Scottish engineer and an Algerian captain. None of them had English as a first language, unless you included (and could understand) Glaswegian.

Billy was escorted, panting and dripping, into the bowels of the ship, into a warm cabin, sparse but comfortable – double bunk, small desk with a chair, and two lockers. It would have been possible, just, to swing a small, short-tailed cat, if it was wearing a crash helmet.

"The head and showers are second door, left. Captain wishes that you remain on this lower deck. You not come up. Here instructions and paper we required give you, on desk. Meals served in cabin." The crewman, in orange overalls a size too big, left without an inscrutable smile, and Billy was left to recover, catch his breath, warm up, and ponder upon the events of the last twelve hours. Had it really only been that short a space of time since ... well, since everything?

He put his rucksack on the top bunk bed, turned, and opened the nearest locker in which he found towels, soap and orange overalls. The other, he found, was empty. He guessed that he was expected to wear the overalls, and was keen to get out of the cold, wet clothes that he had arrived in; he grabbed a towel, soap and underwear from his bag and set off to find the showers. He allowed the hot water to soak into him, and stood in it for a long time. Tiredness overcame him, and he dried himself, dressed in his newly-acquired overalls, and went back to the cabin. Throwing wet clothes in a heap on the floor, he lay down on the bunk, hands behind his head, looking up at the peeling paint on the ceiling: 'Do they have ceilings on ships', he wondered. He slept.

He had no idea what the time was, if it was day or night, how long he had slept for, or, momentarily, who he was or where he was. Then he remembered, and felt a satisfaction in that he had done what he had strived to achieve. He felt justified in righting the wrongs that had been thrust upon him, and briefly, thought about his father and knew he would have been proud of him.

He looked around the cabin, his eyes coming to rest upon a large envelope on the desk. Swinging his legs off the bunk, he had a painful reminder of the fishing boat trip, as his stomach muscles tensed – still suffering from all the retching. With it came the rumbling and hunger from being empty and needing fluid. There was also a little fear and trepidation about the future, the price he would now be expected to pay for the assistance he had been given. He knew where he was going, and what was expected of him in the short term, but it was the longer term that troubled him.

Now standing, he thought how ridiculous he probably looked in the oversize orange overalls. He rolled up the sleeves and the trouser legs – at least now he could walk without standing on his trousers, and no longer felt that he was wearing gloves. He thought about putting his own clothes back on, but, looking around, realised that they had been taken from the cabin.

He sat at the desk, picked up the envelope and turned it over and over, unwilling to open it, knowing that its contents would change his life forever. His life had already changed; he had changed it himself. The envelope was only another stage in it. 'Open the bloody envelope, you idiot', he told himself.

Tearing the end, he emptied the contents, spreading them on the desk. The first sheet he read was a profile of Nick Pile, Belfast University drop-out. He was travelling on (and in) an extended, never ending, gap year. He was 19 years old, born in Reading, orphaned when he was 11, brought (dragged) up in various care homes, and won a place at Uni to do only the first year of an Engineering Degree at QUB. The second sheet was a birth certificate, showing Nick's parents to be Bernard Pile, occupation Bank Clerk, and Betty Pile – Housewife. Discarding that, he picked up a UK Passport showing entry stamps for Tunisia, Algeria and Libya; the date on the last entry was 22nd April 1973. That must be about now, Billy thought, but he realised he didn't actually know what today's date was.

He flicked through the other pages and got to the back, and there he was, it was him; it was his photograph in the passport. He was Nick Pile.

The final sheet of paper from the envelope was hand written. It was short, blunt and to the point, in reasonable English.

You will disembark at the Port of Tripoli at Cargo Berth 6.

You will be meet by a represent of Abuzed Omar Dorda of Mukhababarat el-Jamahiriya. He will take by car to Biraq for education.

You are welcome to our Country

There was a signature at the bottom, which appeared to be Abuzed Omar Dorda, whoever he was. It was covered by an official looking stamp and dated 30th March '73.

Billy, sorry, I mean Nick, didn't know then, but the head of the Libyan Intelligence Service had signed the note, and he reported directly to the man himself, General Muammar Muhammad Abu Minyar al- Gaddafi.

Nick's thoughts were interrupted by a knock on the cabin door – not a normal knock, more like it was being kicked. Opening the door, he met a tray of bowls and dishes being thrust at him by a very small man with an oversized grin, and equally oversized overalls. Strangely, this little man seemed to be almost the same colour as the overalls. Little man didn't speak, just thrust the tray at Nick again, nodded and retreated, closing the door as he left.

Wafts of delicious food smells made his stomach rumble again. He put the tray on the desk, pushing aside the papers and explored the dishes. Rice, hot spicy curry of undetermined ingredients that smelt slightly fishy, skewers of chicken pieces (he'd never had Satay before), a mixture of various vegetables in which he only recognised tomatoes and flat doughy bread of some sort. He attacked it with relish, no I mean with relish. He drank one of the two bottles of water, almost in one. He hadn't realised how thirsty he was.

Nick had lost all sense of time; his watch told him it was 6 o'clock, but he couldn't confidently say if it was morning or evening. His best guess was morning, so he thought he would explore his surroundings a little, and see if he could at least find a porthole to look through. Leaving the cabin door open, thinking it might help him find it again, he walked down the steel-clad corridor, stepping through a bulkhead door and turned right for no reason other than it seemed a reasonable place to start. After a few paces, he was confronted by another door which was closed, and had large, heavy levers top and bottom and a central wheel, which he decided against turning on the basis that it might just be sea water on the other side. Turning away, he was greeted by an orange overall clad figure who shouted at him.

"Back! You go back, you stay in cabin. You not let out."

"Okay, okay." Nick said, holding up his hands. "I understand, it's okay, I just wanted to see outside, I'll go back." He returned to his cabin, watched by the man, until he reached the door. 'I guess I have to put up with my own company, then', he thought, as he closed the door. Sitting at the desk again he contemplated, re-read the papers that he had been left with, and resigned himself to being confined for the rest of the voyage.

Chapter 19

May 1973

"I am Mohammed Abu Al-Barouni, you will wish to call me Mo. You are welcome to my Libya." The smile was broad, genuine and Nick took an instant liking to him. He shook the proffered hand; it was a good grasp, firm and exuded the warmth and sincerity of the words.

It was a great relief to be on solid ground after two weeks on the water; his head still told him that the world was unstable, and he still felt the need to hold onto something solid – rail, post, bench or human hand. The gangway had rocked from side to side as he had descended, but by moving alternate hands down the side ropes, bag on back, he had reached the end to be greeted, almost on his knees, by the smiling, Arab-robed Mo.

To the right, some distance away, a group of uniformed, official-looking people, some with machine pistols slung over shoulders, some with clip-boards, all turned away as Nick disembarked. He assumed these were Customs, Immigration or Police but were clearly following instructions to (literally) 'look the other way'.

"Come!" Mo turned, and walked to the dust covered, white Range Rover. Mo opened the nearest rear door, left it open and walked around to the other side (and near-side, confusing, when you've just got off a boat, and the last car you were in was the right way round). Nick got in, and closed the door, dropping his bag on the floor. The Range Rover took off in a cloud of dust as the 4.2 litre V8 picked up revs and propelled the 4x4 out of the port.

"We have 700 kilometres and our home will be Birak. Your esteemed father, Mister Murphy, has asked that we teach you; our General has instructed, so we will do it and you will be in our family." His broad smile was reassuring, and Nick was comfortable with whatever Mo had in store for him.

The miles flashed by, the sand flashed by – bugger all else flashed by because there was nothing else to flash. 'Thank Christ the car was air conditioned', Nick thought, after a toilet stop – middle of the road, not even pulling into the side, everybody pissing in different directions, no conversation, no sideways looks, just hitch up the robe and get on with it. They got back into the cold car as if nothing had happened. It went on, and on, and he began to wonder what he was heading towards, certainly not civilisation.

Birak was a surprise, though; after six hours of desolate sand, sun, heat and endless bugger all, Birak really was an Oasis Town (nearly a City) in the Desert.

This was his home for the next year.

Mo was his mentor, guide and interpreter. It was Mo who translated the instructions in the handling of Semtex, the preparation of detonators, constructing and assembling a timer, motion detonators, heat sensitive detonators, voice and sound activated detonators. It was Mo who guided him, and instructed him in the assembly and maintenance of the Heckler & Koch HK11, the

Steyer LMG, AK47, M14 and the M1A1 Bazooka and PTRD Anti-Tank weapons. He was already 'proficient' with a variety of handguns, but shooting with Browning, Luger and Colt added to his confidence and expertise. Further 'education' included using codes and ciphers, evasion techniques, defensive driving and the psychology of interrogation.

Training in Birak had been focussed, intense and (almost) all consuming. He had not expected to meet a woman, a soul mate and partner. She was 25, older in many more ways than just age. He learned as much from her as he had from Mo, the Libyan, but not necessarily about combat.

Born in Belgium, Brigitte Albrecht had had a bohemian upbringing, and lived most of her life in Germany. As a student, she gravitated into extreme Left-wing politics and joined the Baader Meinhof Group in 1969. She had been forced to leave Germany after she was identified as being 'involved' in the bombing of a US Army establishment in Heidelberg in May '72. With assistance from East Germany's Stasi (their equivalent to our MI6), she found refuge in Birak, armed with a new identity as Justine Bagot. "It's pronounced Baygo", Justine explained, which is why, right from the start, Nick called her 'Winnie'.

The boring part was the constant questioning of his background, where he was born, who his father was, what his mother's name was, where his sister was, what his dog was called, the colour of his first bike, who he lived with when at University, why he left Uni?

It worked, though; after the year in the desert, he was a suntanned, 20 year old dropout student who had seen the world, sown some wild oats and was ready to go back and face the civilised world.

Chapter 20

May 1973

For me, moving to Devizes was actually a posting to a new Regiment. I was effectively an invalid, of sorts, and did nothing but get fit again whilst I was there, waiting for my discharge. I eventually handed my kit in, and was left alone, spending my time alternating between hospital physio, gym, the many town pubs and the NAAFI, whilst waiting for my discharge date.

I was in the NAAFI bar, alternating between staring at the bottom of a pint glass and the arse of the barmaid, as she bent to get another bag of crisps from the box on the floor (I think I spent more on crisps than beer).

"Do you want another pint, Sam?" I couldn't believe it; out of the blue, Mike, OB, appeared like it was yesterday.

We settled in for a long night of updates, reminisces, outrageous and exaggerated stories, and, Oh yes, a few beers.

"Look, mate, you're just killing time down here, you won't be missed; why don't you come over to my place for a few days and chill?"

I thought long and hard for a millisecond, and we set it up for the beginning of September. 'His place' was actually his parents' holiday cottage that they rarely used. It was on the edge of the Radnor Forrest in Wales, near Bleddfa, a little village that was 'handy' for him being based in Hereford. He would drive like a lunatic to try and break his journey time record of 42 minutes for the 40 odd mile trip. Not easy in those days, but, admittedly, there was less traffic then. OB had turned it into his weekend retreat/love nest/bachelor pad – whatever.

My first visit meant arrival in the dark. I remember getting up in the morning and standing outside the front, and at that time the only, door of the very basic stone shepherd's hut. It was idyllic – a stream running literally past the door, the threshold being a little bridge over it. The smell of the pines and the utter tranquillity and peace of it, I still think of. I spent many hours walking the myriad of paths around the cottage. I have visited several times over the years, sometimes with OB and sometimes alone. He had said: "The key is under the fourth stone to the right of the door, help yourself, but (with a grin), knock if the lights are on."

I just loved the solitude of the place. After his parents died, OB spent a lot of time and money renovating the place, but back then it still had oil lamps and a hand-pump. He retained the wood burner, though, and the whole place had that smoky smell and the blackened beams and paintwork that you would expect.

The approach to the cottage was about half a mile from the village along a steep track, off a sharp bend. The road continued after the stream bridge, and on to Llandrindod and around the Radnor Forest. It was still fairly primitive, in those days, and that September OB and I walked up the mountain to the rim of the slate quarry and around the forest tracks during the day. We ate in the village pub in the evenings, and then retired to sit by the log burner. We put the world to rights, with just a suggestion of alcohol. We both drank cheap brandy and Coke, and would have our own bottle of each. A swig from the brandy bottle would leave room for a top-up of Coke, and this would continue until we ran out of Coke, which always coincided with the draining of the brandy bottle.

The night before I left to go back to Devizes, sitting in front of the crackling fire and before the Brandy kicked in, OB gave me a newspaper, The Irish Times, and a tin of shortbread biscuits. It was a little too heavy to contain biscuits.

"Read the front page"

City Coroner rules Misadventure – charges against RUC quashed.

We were there, so this wasn't a surprise. The article continued, with details of the key witnesses, testimony from the RUC Officers, and explanation of the circumstances regarding identification prior to the arrest. This was attributed to photographs of the deceased at a riot, which had been provided to the RUC by 'Soldier B', which subsequently led to the attempted arrest at a property on the outskirts of Londonderry, known locally as 'The Bogside.'

The date on the paper was two months earlier. OB had written some notes down the side, and had underlined some names in the article, including that of Billy Conlan.

"The word on the street, Sam, is that they (the IRA), will be looking to punish anyone that they think is responsible. This could be a beating, capping, or just 'nine ml under the chin'." OB paused, pushed the tin towards me and continued: "Your name is NOT out there, but... 'Speccy Five Eyes' is, and it's clear from the report that he is, or was 'Soldier B'. Put that (nodding at the tin), somewhere safe, you might need it one day."

Chapter 21

July 1974

Billy (now Nick Pile), was sweating, nervous, agitated and tried to calm himself as he waited in the queue. Looking around, he tried to spot other people who were travelling alone. Maybe he could start a conversation, and then walk out through Immigration with them, so that he wouldn't look so suspicious. He gave himself a mental talking to: 'Get a grip, take some deep breaths, and look like you're relaxed'.

The clock on the wall told him that local time was 20:33. He thought it odd that he had been travelling for two days; Birak to Algeria 1000 miles by road, then eight hours in airports and on planes, Algeria to Manchester via Amsterdam and he was still in the same time zone. Research back in Birak had shown this to be the route (and airline), least likely to create a 'troubled' arrival in Manchester. He had slept for a couple of hours on the plane from Houari to Schiphol, and he was wide-awake, buzzing, and it felt like early morning.

He followed the snake trail of the queue to Immigration. The queue split several ways just ahead, and he chose the booth from which, four ahead of him in the line, a passenger had just been 'escorted' back into a side room. It was a spur of the moment decision – just seemed that the Passport Control guy might still have his mind elsewhere. He was right; his passport received merely a cursory glance, the officer watching (over Nick's shoulder), the events in the area around the side room where a scuffle had broken out, a second passenger having joined the first.

He walked past the booth and on, following the other passengers, following the baggage claim signs, and choosing a less crowded part of the baggage hall, he waited for the carrousel to start. He was relieved to have negotiated Immigration so well, and was pleased with his reading of the situation. This had been a significant part of his training: study the surroundings, read the signals, the body language, assess, move decisively and confidently.

The carrousel started, and he watched for his bag. It seemed ages before his appeared, and the crowd around the belt had diminished considerably when he grabbed his, slung it over his shoulder and marched confidently (he thought), out of the hall, along the twists and turns of the corridors – no sense of direction, just following the arrows.

Selecting the 'Nothing to Declare' route, he was unchallenged, not even the sniffer dog sniffed. The arrivals hall was crowded at the entrance, and he had to shoulder his way through hugging, tearful travellers and greeters who were oblivious to their surroundings and dropped luggage, just intent on the 'welcome home'. He was slightly envious, and a bit sad that he was alone, but also elated in that he was out and clear. He was free and anonymous; a nobody, who was unidentified and unidentifiable.

He walked out of the hall, detouring only to cash a Travellers Cheque, he chose the nearest exit; he stepped out into the warm, wet dusk of a Manchester evening in July 1974.

The preparation had been brilliant, flawless in the documentation, the background that had been created for him, the organisation that had enabled him to change his identity, and the structured 'education' programme that he had had. This was no 'bogtrotter' organisation; this was a serious, undercover operation. He was inspired by it, confident of his cover, focused, organised and very much in control, but understandably 'nervous'.

The address had been memorised, and he told the taxi driver where he wanted to go. He had a new, untried cheque book, and now £100 cash – the hand full of Libyan Dinar he had thrown into the charity bucket. The trip was uneventful. Four quid to Stockport was a bit over the top, but he did not want to be memorable and argue, so gave him five and said, "Keep it buddy", as he got out at the terraced house. Number 27 was nondescript, average, boring, uninspiring, and unmemorable; everything he needed it to be.

The door was unlocked, as arranged, and he dropped his bag as the door clicked shut behind him and explored.

Living room to the left, stairs to the right, kitchen ahead, cloak room and toilet built as an extension. At the back was a rear exit off the side of the kitchen into a small yard – a solid door at the end. This led onto a large car park with the rear of the shops, offices and take-aways that faced the high street beyond. This will work for me, he thought.

Back in the kitchen, and there was a note from the letting agent, an inventory to sign and the landlord's contact details. The junk mail went into the bin, and he went up the stairs, collecting his bag as he went. There was a small bedroom to the left front with another slightly larger at the front. The right of the bedrooms led to the bathroom that was over the kitchen, with the flat roof of the extension visible from the window, and then the car park.

Entering the front bedroom, he emptied the contents of his bag on the double bed, and stood for a while at the window, looking up and down the empty street. It was getting dark now, and streetlights were beginning to light up. He could see the television flickering in the ground floor window of the house opposite. It was a scene of total normality and anonymity.

His stomach growled, reminding him that he needed food. Leaving everything where it lay, he left the house through the back door, and went into and across the car park to explore the high street food options, and consider the next move – to find a job.

The small Chinese restaurant was not busy, with only one other table occupied; the couple sitting at it were oblivious to the world. At the front was a small seating area, with red, plastic, faux leather benches for waiting take-away customers. They had been provided with a selection of magazines and papers amongst which he found Manchester Evening News dated Tuesday 11th June – that day. He scooped it up as he was shown to a table, and, after a quick look at the menu, ordered and scanned the jobs pages. His King Prawn Curry with Fried Rice arrived, and he asked if he could borrow a pen.

His meal was a mix of fork fulls and circled jobs – the pen replacing the fork at the wrong time, occasionally.

He asked for the bill, left £3 and the pen on the table; it was well over the top as a tip, so he felt entitled to take the paper with him. The paper now had various jobs circled, and phone numbers underlined. He needed to work fast; although he had a £500 bank balance, he would need a car, and would have rent to pay after the first month. He was tasked with establishing himself in every respect within a week of arrival before reporting in and 'going live'.

Chapter 22

July 1974

The interview was short, hardly even a formality; a photocopy of his licence and a form to sign authorising a security check – and he had a job. He was now officially employed as a van delivery driver for Ad-Van-Tage Distribution Ltd, based in a simple warehouse in Stockport. AVT received consignments at around midnight, sorted them into vanloads ready for distribution the next day around Manchester, Lancashire and the North West of England.

Nick soon got into the routine: start time 6am. Load his van in reverse delivery order, first drop loaded last, and usually rolling by 7:30. Deliveries varied, but could be up-to 30 drops per day. A lot were 'regulars', and he quickly learned the short cuts, rat runs, and back alleyways that shaved a couple of minutes here and there. Initially, he was not getting back to the warehouse until 5 o'clock. As the days passed, and he became more familiar with the area, roads and the times when he knew the customers would be in to receive parcels, and the shift end time came down to 3:30ish. He really enjoyed the job, and was quite confident that he would fit his 'extra' activities around it.

He had been left alone to establish his credibility in the work place, but was considered to be 'a loner', and a bit antisocial. He didn't go for a pint with the other lads, didn't meet anyone after work, and just kept himself to himself. His only regular routine was to call at the same newsagents every evening on his way home to buy the Manchester Evening News. Once safely home, he would put the kettle on, turn straight to the Small Ads, scan them and bin the paper unread. It was nearly six weeks before he saw the first advert.

LOST DOG –
Irish Wolfhound lost in the Stockport area.

Answers to the name Murphy.
Please call 01869734710.

He knew the numbers were right, just not in that order. At 7 o'clock, the prescribed time, he dialled the number and waited, with not just a little trepidation.

"Yes?", the voice said after four rings.

"This is Murphy." Nick said.

"Everything okay?", said the voice.

"Fine." said Nick. And so it began.

It was basically a vehicle delivery job – a train ride to Liverpool, collect the van, drive down the motorway to Birmingham. Park where he was told to park, lock it, put the key in the envelope, and drop it into the post-box, catch the train home, job done.

A week later, he drove to Manchester Airport, parked in the short-stay car park and made his way into the arrivals hall and waited, watching the arrivals board impatiently. A tired Winnie emerged from the arrivals' exit, looking left and right until she spotted him, smiling and tearful. She looked stunning; tanned and slim. They stood for a long minute between suitcases –

hugged, kissed and hugged some more. He didn't want to let go of her, but was slightly nervous and wary of any surveillance or interest either of them may have attracted. Taking the largest case, he said: "The car's just across the road, you must be hungry"…

"I'm hungry for you!" She said, and, linking arms and almost legs, they walked out into late afternoon sunshine.

Work was getting easier, and Nick was settled, comfortable with the routine until…

Summoned to the traffic office, he was confronted with the forms to sign. It was explained that: "We've got a new drop at the airport, and we've got to get security clearance for all the drivers, so we got to do a CRB check on everyone; you got any problem with that, Nick?"

"Er, no. No problem."

"OK, mate, just sign here and we'll get it sorted." The phone rang; Nick signed the form, and left as the phone conversation continued. He was a little concerned that this Criminal Record check might throw up something, but, thinking about it, it shouldn't if his ID held up. He waited, and, after two uncomfortable weeks, his clearance came through – a new ID Photo Card around his neck and his security pass, and he could deliver 'air-side' at the Airport, St Mary's Hospital and the University.

As the months passed, Nick and Winnie settled into domesticity, and outwardly lived a quiet, settled life in suburban North Cheshire, on the outskirts of Manchester. They had few friends, did not socialise, and were largely anonymous. The few people that knew them were aware that they had frequent trips 'away', visiting several cities and towns on day trips and sometimes weekend stays.

Nick was religious in his routine of collecting the Manchester Evening News. Winnie was a good, competent driver, and always stayed within the law in terms of speed, parking and never drew attention to herself or her vehicle. As a consequence, dropping Nick off at Stranraer, Liverpool, Holyhead or wherever his vehicle collection point was, was never logged on any Police database.

The 'Lockup' was the biggest risk, and they took great measures to minimise attention whenever they visited it. Nick had rented it under an assumed name, picked at random from the phone book. They left it empty for some time before taking the first 'consignment'. He made sure that it was secure, access unobserved, and always visited at times when he knew others wouldn't be around.

The 'up and over' garage door exposed a bench, some cheap tools and a jumble of car parts, bike wheels, two steel filing cabinets (empty), an old bed frame, several garden chairs, a pile of timber off-cuts, and, leaning against the rear wall, a smelly and stained double mattress. There was very little room to walk through the garage, and getting to the rear involved clambering over (and through), what could only be described as 'junk'. Squeezing past a smelly mattress was not for the faint hearted, but it revealed a door through the stud partition wall at the rear that was only apparent with a tape measure. The external length of the garage was 28 feet, the internal 24. The 4 feet beyond the mattress was pristine, almost clinical and contained the entire stock of mainland based munitions of the IRA. This was Nick's domain; he had devoted almost half his life to the creation of this resource – weapons, ammunition, det-cord, timers and block-stacked at one end, almost one tonne of Semtex blocks, enough to remove Stockport from Cheshire, and deposit it over the Pennines in Leeds.

It was here that Nick constructed his devices; this was his workshop, his studio. This is where he performed, where he practised his art, the creation of the horrific, deadly devices that killed maimed and injured so many.

Chapter 23

June 1995

His instructions were clear, brief, but detailed, and everything he needed to carry out the task. It included the exact time that the coded warning would be given.

The three tonne truck was parked, just as he was told it would be, on the retail park in Irlam. Winnie dropped him off outside the Supermarket, and he trudged, collar up, shoulders down, dejected, miserable, projecting the image. It was nine o'clock in the evening, dark now, raining, Manchester.

The keys were on the offside front tyre, the tank full – ready to roll. He unlocked, climbed into the cab and had a quick play with the unfamiliar controls, started up and drove off. He knew the ultimate destination, but first, drove to the lorry park at the Trafford Park Industrial area. Here, it was just another truck; he was just another weary trucker resting before the next delivery. He parked next to a Refer (a refrigerated trailer), its top mounted generator rumbling on, masking any noise that he would make whilst assembling everything in the back of his truck.

Switching on the rear load compartment lights, he got out of the cab, opened the rear door of the truck, and climbed up, pulling the door closed behind him.

There were two pallets, each containing 40 sacks of Nitrogen fertiliser (two tonnes in total), a stack of Semtex blocks, that he estimated to be about 300 kilos, several detonators and a box of wire coils, batteries and timers. Until connected, stable, inert, (almost) harmless. He smiled, rubbed his hands together in anticipation; he was at home, comfortable with this kit. This was his area of expertise, and he was going to be creative.

He slept in the cab along with all the other truckers that were parked around him. At eight o'clock, he started the engine, and moved slowly out of the parking area onto the main road into Manchester, Deansgate and the shopping area. The delivery docks were under the shopping centre with a one-way system, barriers at both ends, but the inbound security office and barrier was unattended. That won't happen again after today, he thought. He had delivered here before, knew the routine and how pathetic the security was. They seemed to be fairly good at stopping exiting vehicles to check things weren't being nicked, and didn't consider checking on what was being delivered. He backed onto the dock for DG Sports, ignored the shop's rear doorbell, and walked four doors down to Serious Kitchen Supplies and rang their bell. A quick check on his watch showed he had fourteen minutes before the phone call.

The door opened, and a young girl with a frown and puzzled expression said: "We haven't got a delivery today."

"No, I'm not delivering to you, love, but I can't get an answer from DG. Can I just nip through to the front and give 'em a kick?" Nick said, putting on his most charming smile.

She looked at his healthy suntan, smile, white teeth, twinkle in his eye and, thoughts elsewhere, fluttered and said: "Sure, come on in."

She half opened the shutter at the front for him, and he bent under it and said: "Thanks love, I hope I can do your delivery one day."

She smiled and said: "No probs, I'll look forward to it."

Now, out into the main shopping area, he stuffed his hands into his pockets and shuffled, miserable, head down, fed-up and not looking forward to his day's work in retail, he made his way to the entrance (in his case exit). He paused until a group of people approached the security guard to show their entry passes, and squeezed passed the group going in the opposite direction.

The security system was designed to vet people coming in before opening time, not going out, and he was not challenged. Now, out on the street, he started to walk away as the alarms started, sirens in the distance, approaching. It was now another nine minutes before the time he had set, which would be twenty two minutes after the warning telephone call that had been made to the Daily Mail news desk, along with the code of the day 'Winston Churchill'. Code words were agreed on a daily basis by Home Office (via RUC) and the IRA. The call had been considered a 'credible' threat; all emergency services were alerted and tasked with clearing the area as fast as possible.

As he walked towards the main road, a police car, blue lights and sirens bouncing of the buildings shot passed the junction ahead. He caught a flash of brake lights, and instantly turned and began to slowly walk back towards the shopping centre that he had just left. Thirty seconds later, the police car slithered to a halt beside him and the passenger window descended.

"Where are you going, sunshine?"

"I'm going to work," with a gesticulation towards the building, "In there, and I'm late. Why? What's going on?"

"There's a problem this morning; we've had a bomb alert. Turn around, and get as far away from here as you can. You, sunshine, have got the day off. You and everyone else who works in there." The window rolled up, the car shot off, and Nick turned around (again), and continued to walk away.

The main street was full of people all going in the same direction, and, strangely, no traffic at all. Some were running, a few stood discussing what was happening, confusion, disbelief, and, obviously decisions being made. Should we go and have a coffee whilst they sort this out, or should we just say, 'sod it', and go home?

The blast wave hit before the sound wave.

It was seven minutes before the warning said it would be. Police were still ushering people away, and, along with the security staff, some were still trying to clear the building. Outside, people were knocked off their feet; windows blew out, glass shards and fragments cutting through anything and everything including bodies. Dust was billowing and swirling around… and then came the sound of the massive explosion. As their hearing returned, the momentary silence was replaced by cries of pain and fear, tinkling of glass, the thud of masonry, whimpers and quiet moans, shrieks of pain and shocked sobbing, only then to be drowned by the sirens, alarms and the sound of demolition. The dust clouds continued moving slowly up the main road, leaving behind rubble and bricks, litter, dropped possessions, uneaten breakfast and packed lunches. Amongst it all, an opportunist dog had his nose buried in a carrier bag.

Seventeen people died. One hundred and four people were injured; of these, six lost limbs.

Chapter 24

February 1998

The meeting had been arranged for March but, at the 'request' of the Home Secretary, had been brought forward. It was to be held at the Home Office, Queen Anne's Gate, Westminster. Attending the meeting were representatives from Michael Howard's Office (Home Secretary), Patrick Mayhew's Office (NI Minister) and Sir Ian Spedding's Office (SIS Chief of Staff). Also present, were representatives from the RUC, British Army and Metropolitan, Greater Manchester and Merseyside Police Forces.

The meeting was preceded by very, very close scrutiny of identification credentials, and then coffee, before the assembled 'high level' delegates were ushered into the darkened meeting room. Although ten in the morning, blinds were drawn – all light and intrusion minimised.

A cheery, "Good morning Ladies and Gentlemen; I represent The Home Secretary, welcome to the Home Office. Can we start by asking you to introduce yourselves, by identifying the department that you each represent, without the need for personal introductions?" And, turning to his left and looking down (in more ways than one), said: "Can we go round the table; perhaps you would like to start?"

In a clear, hard, Ulster accent, the ruddy-faced, perspiring, nameless person disclosed that he represented the Royal Ulster Constabulary, Belfast. The ritual continued around the table, ending back where it started.

"The Home Secretary has tasked us with eliminating an IRA Cell that has been responsible for many acts of terrorism, deaths and carnage on the streets of several cities on the UK Mainland. The UK Police Forces have evidence that links several of the incidents, and it is our strong belief that only one Cell is responsible for most, if not all, of the terrorist attacks of the last decade. Our RUC colleagues believe that they have now identified the leader of this group, and also have infiltrated the Ireland- based command structure that controls this group. I'll leave it to our RUC representative to give you the background details".

He sat, and looked to the RUC man on his left, but, to his right, Roisin Docherty surprised everyone by standing; she was at the far end of the table and began to speak in a clear, un-wavering, confident voice.

"At the height of 'the troubles' in the late 1960's, a young man, trained and indoctrinated by the IRA, shot and killed, in a very brutal way, five people from two families in the North of Ireland. He then vanished". Pausing to look down at a file, she opened it, extracted copies of crime scene photographs, and several other documents, some of which she passed to her left and then to her right, to be distributed. She waited, whilst the assembled group had chance to take in the horrendous images, waited for sharp intakes of breath, revulsion, horror, vomiting or any other extreme reaction. She was disappointed; these were hardened veterans, not unused to seeing the results of man's inhumanity.

"We have statements from survivors of these brutal killings. Document seven is a statement made by Helen Carroll, the surviving daughter of a murdered RUC officer, and the subsequent identification made from photographs shown to her of our suspect.

Document nine is the statement made by Maddie Ford, the only survivor of the killing of three other family members and her photo ID statement. Both witnesses identified the same man, who we believe to be one Billy Conlan, formally a resident of Londonderry, who vanished the day after the killings in 1968.

We have recently matched fingerprints from a car we believe was used by the killer at that time, to explosive devices that failed to detonate in Birmingham last year, and to a vehicle that we believe was used to transport explosives to Colchester, Essex earlier this year. It was abandoned in close proximity to an explosion. We suspect that it was the intention to include the destruction of this vehicle in that explosion. We have photographs of the suspect taken around the time of the Ireland killings when he was 20, in 1973; document thirteen shows an artist's impression of what we would expect him to look like today, aged 42. We know that he has a new identity; we don't know who he is now; we don't know where he is now, but...." Long pause from Roisin, and looking around the assembled faces, continued, "We are convinced that this is the leader of the Cell that we need to find".

"Do we have any sightings at all after '73?" All faces turned to the questioner, who had previously identified himself as being 'A member of the armed forces'.

"No, nothing", Roisin said. "All we can do is circulate his prints, and what we think he might look like now, and hope that we can drag something out of the woodwork that we can pursue".

"Do we have anyone 'out-there' that knew him back in the 70s"? It was a voice from the other end of the table, an SIS voice. Field Officer David (Dodge) Rogers was an NI veteran, and had been on active service in several 'theatres'. "It occurs to me that we must have had guys out there then that would have some knowledge of the main players. Is our man showing on any intel then, or are there any leads to other connections, family, friends, girls, interests? A 20 year old lad in Londonderry must leave a trace, even if it's only semen?" There was a silence, whilst the assembled stuffed shirts composed themselves.

"What my colleague is saying has some validity, albeit indelicately illustrated", said an unidentified 'spook', wearing a strangely old fashioned bow-tie; he was obviously more refined.

There was a gathering of thoughts, eventually interrupted by RUC Deputy Chief Constable Robert Litt: "We all had people on the ground then, who either came into contact with this man, or came into contact with people who knew him, even if they didn't know that they did, if you know what I mean."

Colonel George Bennett (22 Regiment SAS), picked up the photograph, statement files and artist's pictures and shuffled them from hand to hand. The action drew attention from everyone, and there was an expectant focus on him. He spread the papers on the table in front of him, and, lining up the edges of each page, spread his hands on the table and sat back with a sigh. "We had assets on the ground in '73 who will have known of this suspect". He moved the papers closer together to more accurately align the corners, and continued: "I'm confidant that they will build a picture of who he was, who he is most likely to be now, but... the guys on the ground then are now also 20 years older- so don't expect miracles."

Chapter 25

April 1998

It was still raining and cold; the wind was blowing off the sea, and Phil Neath could taste the salt. Leaving the warmth of the car, now exposed to the elements, he pulled the collar of his jacket up, crouched slightly, and hurried across the pad to the waiting Mk7 Lynx. He was helped into it by a crewman, and, with a howl as the rotors began to turn, he settled (sort-of) into the aluminium-framed, canvas seat that he was pointed to. Now strapped in, within seconds, he felt the vibration, as the pilot eased back on the collective, adjusted the cyclic, tap-danced, patted his head and rubbed his tummy … and the Lynx was up, and leaving the twinkling lights of Belfast behind them.

There was no in-flight entertainment, no safety lecture, no refreshments; this was a workhorse, more like sitting in the back of a truck than in a taxi. Flight time to Hereford was just over an hour, 200 miles – just enough time for the seat to become uncomfortable, legs to start going numb, and ears to start bleeding from the noise if it didn't end soon.

He had been 'summoned' to attend a meeting, didn't know why, didn't know what it was about. His head of department at the Belfast office of UK Trade and Investment (UKTI) had walked into his office and said:

"Just drop everything; there's a car waiting to take you to the harbour heli-pad. George Bennett has asked for you to nip over – seems to be some sort of panic job."

Although UKTI was a government agency which helped anyone who wanted to develop overseas markets, Phil's 'day job' was actually managing a group of highly skilled undercover field officers who were infiltrating various IRA Battalions in both the north and south of Ireland. He had left the Regiment five years earlier, and, although now working for SIS, he still had close connections with Hereford, as some of his operatives were regiment lads. He knew George well, and had confidence in him, knowing that he would not be wasting his or anyone else's time.

Unusually, George himself met him on the tarmac at the edge of the parade ground. George was accompanied, at discrete distance, by a uniformed and armed soldier that Phil didn't know, and wasn't introduced to. He ducked under the rotor wash, and they shook hands, walking to the admin block, as the Lynx took off again, preventing any conversation. The quiet of the corridor they were in was a startling contrast to the noise of the last hour, and Phil initially started shouting rather than talking.

"Good to see you, George. What's up?"

"Tea, Phil? Come on in." He followed Colonel Bennett into the office, who continued with: "I think you already know this chap? I won't bother with introductions."

"OB! How the devil are you? Been a few years." Mike O'Brian stood, grinning, tanned, and slightly greying, with close-cropped hair, scruffy jeans and trainers. They shook hands.

"I'm well, Phil, ta! You don't look in bad nick for an old' en. I won't give you the bullshit about not looking any older; you do, but remember, you're still older than me."

"First things first." Phil said, turning to George: "My taxi has just buggered off, does that mean I'm stuck here?"

"I'm not sure yet, Phil, it depends on what you old guys can remember. Then we'll decide what happens next." Phil shot a quizzical look at OB.

"Don't look at me mate; he hasn't told me what's going on yet either."

Tea arrived, and George said: "Thanks, Jack; shut the door for me, please." Jack handed mugs to Phil and Mike, leaving the tray and sugar on the desk. They exchanged nods of thanks and the door closed with a click signifying that explanations could begin.

George bent slightly, and retrieved a thick file and two large envelopes from the bottom right-hand drawer, dropping them with a theatrical slap on his desk. Leaving them where they landed, he leaned back and, looking over the heads of Phil and Mike, he began his explanation.

"Since 1975ish, there have been a series of 'incidents', 32 to be exact, all of which have been attributed to the IRA. These range from letter bombs, to large-scale outrageous incidents like the Manchester bombing. They include unexplained fatal traffic 'accidents', and questionable suicides. There have been attacks on Army establishments and personnel, and the bombing of pubs frequented by military families. Some of these incidents have common elements, and we think we have identified an IRA operative who is responsible. We think he has been on the mainland for some time, is deeply embedded, skilled, and resourceful – and we can't find him.

We don't know who he is, or who he is working with. However, we know who he was. He left prints at bomb scenes in the last couple of months, which match some left in a car back in '73." George paused and, retrieving the envelopes, he handed one to each of the men who leaned forward in unison to collect them.

Opening the envelopes, removing documents, statements and photographs, it was OB who reacted first: "Bloody Hell! That's Billy One!", he exclaimed.

"Well," George said, "Back in 1973, he was Billy Conlan, who killed five members of two families in Ulster, and then vanished. We think he is leading this Cell; we don't know what support or resources he has over here, but we think he follows instructions from over the water. What do you know about him, Mike?"

OB related the story of Billy's family, the death of his mother, father, the inquest and the subsequent murders that were attributed (in his absence) to Billy 'One' Conlan.

"But what do you know about him since then, any clues to who he might be now, where he went to from 'Derry?"

"Not a clue, George." Turning to Phil: "Do you remember him?"

"No, but I remember the incident and the inquest. There was a lot of interest and media coverage, and, to an extent, that increased the outcry of injustice, and outraged the locals – there were all sorts of threats at the time about retribution and revenge. I think Billy kept quite a low profile. It was all the IRA hard men that were doing all the shouting. I remember the riots that night with Bernadette (Devlin) spouting off at Free 'Derry Corner."

"Any known associates, Phil?"

"None I know of, George. Billy wasn't really on my radar."

"Mike?"

"No, George; as you know I was shipped out to sun and sand in '74."

Phil tried (unsuccessfully), to suppress a yawn, and, with a glance up at the clock, George said: "I've booked you both into The Dragon. It's 8 now, and the restaurant stops taking orders at 9:30, so I'd better let you go. Jack will give you 'survival packs', and I'll see you back here at 9 tomorrow. We have a meeting with some other interested parties from London and Belfast."

As if by magic, Jack appeared at the door and everyone stood. "Sorry I can't join you for a drink; I've got another meeting." George said. They shook hands, turned to the waiting Jack, and left the office clutching their envelopes, "Mike!" George called, and pausing, OB turned. "I know you still have sand in your trainers, but I don't want you to give the wrong impression tomorrow." OB grinned, nodded and caught up with Jack and the trailing Phil.

Chapter 26

April 1998

The Green Dragon was a well-used town centre hotel, pub, bar, and was known by both men. The Ford Granada, driven very rapidly by Jack, dropped them at the door clutching identical (courtesy of Jack) hold-alls, but OB also having a Burgan over one shoulder.

Phil held the door for Mike.

"Hi Mike, not seen you for months." The receptionist was clearly pleased to see him. She smiled at Phil, but quickly returned to Mike, all fluttering eyes, almost, but not quite, discrete, almost panting, almost drooling – but trying hard to keep control. "I saw your name on the booking, so I stayed on for a bit".

Leaning his six-foot two frame over the reception desk, Mike air kissed both cheeks, and said: "Looking good as ever, Hannah", and, as they both looked her straight in the cleavage, he said: "We need to shower, eat and talk for a bit, but if you're still around, perhaps we can have a drink later?"

"I should be, Mike; I'll be in the bar later, and I'll keep an eye out for you." She did a pirouette, sweeping up keys and cards in a fluid movement, handing Phil a set: "You're in 53, Mister Neath", and, turning to Mike: "And you are in 51, Mister O'Brian." It was a slightly longer key hand-over, and there was a moment where

Phil thought he should suggest he met OB for breakfast. "Could you complete the registration cards and drop them back to reception, please? Thank you. It's *really* good to see you, Mike." Another smile, and, as they gathered bags and keys, they headed towards the lift.

Mike turned as they left and said, "See you later, love."

In the lift Phil said nothing but grinned at OB. After a pause, Mike returned the grin: "What?"

"Nothing mate, nothing at all." Phil replied, with an exaggerated wink.

"Right, shall we say the bar in twenty minutes then?"

Phil's room was nondescript, comfortable, and adequate, and he dropped the bag on the bed and explored the bathroom. Turning the shower on, he emptied the bag on the bed, opened the toothbrush packet, stripped and returned to the bathroom and showered. He stood under the hot water and let the heat and steam relax his muscles, thought about the meeting with George, and speculated upon tomorrow's meeting, the history and the past life of Billy Conlan.

Twenty minutes had already passed by the time he got out of the shower and dried himself. The bag contained T shirts, dark tan chinos, socks and underwear – all still wrapped and new, all his size. He smiled at the efficiency, detail and forethought that had been involved in creating the 'survival pack' that George had organised. His shoes didn't quite go with the chinos, but he thought he looked ok. Putting his suit jacket back on, he collected the envelope and left the room to find Mike in the bar.

Hannah was sitting on a stool at the bar, her back to the door, with Mike leaning on one elbow, glass in hand, standing very close to her. He stopped talking as Phil walked across the room towards them, and patted Hannah on the hand that was resting on his knee. She turned, glanced at Phil, slid fluidly off the stool, and left with a quick peck on Mike's cheek.

"What do you want, Phil?"

"I'll have a pint of … no, I'll have a large Shiraz please Mike."

"Let's eat, and we can talk in the restaurant; it's quieter in there." Food was ordered, and the glass of wine order changed to a bottle. With pauses for delivery by various waitresses, they talked.

"What are your thoughts, then?" Phil asked. "If Billy One *is* the man, he's well hidden and won't be easy to find. Let's assume that the guys looking for him know what they are doing. They haven't found him in nearly twenty bloody years, so we'll have to do something a bit different if we're going to find him".

"Do you remember Sam Burgess, Phil?"

"Er, name's familiar – remind me."

"He was with me in Crossmaglen, but you had him in Hereford in sixty-something".

"Oh yes, I remember him; a bit wet, not regiment stuff, but quite tough in his own way. I drew the short straw, and was told that I had to get him up to speed to go dark for some army role as a photographer, I think, is that right, have I got the right bloke?"

"Yeah, that's him; he was my partner for a while at XMG. We did a few stags together, and then he was seconded to the RUC. He was instrumental in the big RUC inquiry case when they were under the cosh about Billy One's mother being killed after a bungled arrest in 'Derry. He was targeted by the IRA after the inquest along with the coroner and several others, all of whom they think were killed by Billy. I warned Sam off, told him to keep his head down, 'coz they didn't know who he was other that his stupid street name, 'Speccy Five Eyes'. I don't know what's happened to him, or where he is now; we've sort of lost touch, but we were good mates for a while, and used to meet up now and then for a drink and a natter"

"What's this got to do with finding Billy One?"

"Well, I was just thinking, if it really is Billy out there, the way to flush him out would be to use Sam."

"How would Sam know where he is, Mike?"

"You're being thick, mate; I mean telling Billy where Sam is, not asking Sam where Billy is."

"And you think Sam would be up for it?"

"Not if he is sane, no. But if we leak his location to our friends across the water, we could wait for Billy to turn up, fairly simple really."

"Got it. So, you think if I get Sam's ID and whereabouts leaked through my guys in Ireland that it would get filtered through to Billy, and he would want to have a go at Sam?"

"That's exactly what I'm thinking, but it has some serious risks, and I don't know if Bennett would go for it. Don't know if whoever is jerking Bennett around would go for it either, but I can't think of another way, can you?" Phil emptied his glass, poured another, leaned back and thought about what OB had said. He looked across the dining room and saw Hannah. His mind wandered momentarily, and was jealous of his friend's obvious 'second course'.

"Let me think about it, Mike. I have to be sure that my contacts over there would not be compromised by feeding any of this sort of stuff through UKTI. I'm knackered, mate. I need to get some sleep." Draining his glass, and, looking again at Hannah, he stood, smiled and said, "I'll leave you to have your night-cap."

Chapter 27

April 1998

Jack was outside the Hotel at eight forty as arranged, parking the Granada on double yellow lines, and without a disabled badge.

Mike was a little bleary-eyed, had managed to get to breakfast on time, but with little time or inclination to talk in any great depth about the project that Colonel George Bennett had given them. Hurried orange juice, bacon and eggs, and coffee had left them little time to formulate a plan, but Phil had an idea from the previous night's conversation what his friend had in mind.

"I've been thinking", Mike finally said, in the car, en route to the meeting with whoever they were to meet.

"Thinking what?"

"How old are you now, Phil?"

"You know how old I am."

"So, just humour me, how old are you?"

"I'm 51, which makes you 50, yeah? So, your point is?"

"Well, I've been thinking, Sam Burgess is about our age, and is not going to relate to any of the pricks that we have to deal with nowadays. We're all old blokes now, not field ops anymore, God knows what Sam's been up to over the years; he could be in a wheelchair for all we know. I don't think he is, but he's an old bloke now, like you", grinning. "So, whatever we come up with, and we both know what that is likely to be, it will mean that *WE* will have to front it with Sam. He won't trust anyone else. Shit, let's face it, he probably won't even trust us."

"And the answer is?"

"Well, I thought about it a lot last night".

"At what point between your thrusting was that, then?"

"No, fuck off, Phil, I'm being serious now. I don't think we should tell Sam what we are doing at this stage." There was silence for a while, whilst Phil digested the implications of Mike's suggestion.

After a set of traffic lights, a McDonald's and a Sainsbury's corner shop, Phil exploded: "You mean that you think we should con Sam into doing this; con him into giving his agreement, without telling him about the risks of involvement? Are you saying we should not tell him that we are setting him up as a fucking target? Are you fucking serious? You mean don't tell him at all, Mike, is that what you're saying?" There was silence in the car. Nothing more was said.

They were stopped at the gates by the usual security checks; these were dealt with through Jack's customary efficiency, dismissing the formalities with a familiarity that showed the importance of both his passengers, and his status. They arrived at the office block, and were met at the door by a uniformed Staff Sergeant. "Sorry to do this, Gents, but I have to go through the procedures." That meant patting down and a 'wand' between the legs and around backs.

"This is serious shit; do you think we've just got off a boat from Banana Land?" Mike said. Phil cringed at the inappropriate comment, but they passed through, and were directed to a conference room, not as they expected, to George's office. Clearly, this meeting was to be far more "formal" than the previous one with George.

"Good morning, chaps". George Bennett said, as he stood to greet the duo as they entered the conference room. "Get yourselves a coffee, and I'll introduce you. This is Detective Inspector Maynard, Greater Manchester Police." Nods were exchanged as cups were filled, and Mike and Phil surveyed the assembled faces. Colonel Bennett continued with the introductions: "SIS Field Officer Rogers, SIS Officer, and principle Home Office liaison, Philip Stuart-Rae, Bob Lit RUC Chief Constable".

More nods were exchanged, and they took their places around the long table. "I've already told everyone who you guys are, and we'll keep this as informal as we can – so this is Mike and Phil, gentleman. I understand that Mike is already known to you, Dave." Again, nods were exchanged, and George headed to the board that occupied almost the entire end wall of the room. "I'm not going to go over everything again, because you are all up to speed with where we are at, but..." He paused, looked around at the faces, and then continued dramatically "...I can tell you that a bomb was detonated in Birmingham last night that is attributed to our man; it has his MO all over it. It's imperative that we find those responsible as a matter of utmost urgency, 'no stone unturned', 'no matter what it takes', is the word from the Home Office." He glanced at Philip Stuart-Rea. "So, Phil, Mike, you're effectively our 'fresh eyes'; what are your thoughts?"

Mike and Phil exchanged glances, Phil shaking his head almost imperceptively, but it was noticed by George, who raised an eyebrow, and waited for a further reaction from him that was not forthcoming.

"We have a possible avenue", Mike said, and, leaning back in his chair, continued: "It's probably fair to say that Phil and I have some differences over this, but let me lay it out for you, and then Phil can list the problems as he sees them". Another exchange of glances, and this time, a nod from Phil, and Mike continued. "Back in the late sixties, Phil and I both had dealings with an Army guy, Sam Burgess who wasn't 'Regiment', but worked with us, and then worked for the RUC. He featured in a big Court case that subsequently led to Billy Conlan going on his killing spree – before he disappeared. He took out the Coroner and most of his family, the Arresting Officer and his family, and the only one on his hit list that he didn't get to was the guy we worked with a couple of years earlier.

At the time, he was referred to in court as Soldier B, but everyone, including the bad guys, knew him as 'Speccy Five Eyes'. He got this name on the streets in 'Derry because he wore little, round, steel-rimmed glasses and had a camera almost permanently in front of his nose". There was a murmur of anticipation, and almost excitement from the three attentive listeners. Mike continued: "Phil and I agree that we could use Sam to flush out our man. We don't quite agree on the methodology, though. I think that we will only get one shot at this, and we can't afford not to have Sam on board. The issue we have...", with a nod to Phil, and turning directly to face him, he went on: "I don't want to ask for Sam's help and run the risk of being turned down – because we then have nowhere to go. I want to put our arms around him, keep him real close … and then leak his ID and address to the bad guys."

There was silence, and all eyes turned to Phil who studied the faces, trying to gauge reaction. "You don't need to say anything, Phil." George said, putting both hands flat on the table. "I know the ethics of this are all wrong; this is a comrade, an ex-comrade if you prefer, but this is not what we do. You, Mike, are suggesting that we effectively stake him out as bait, without telling him, set him up in the most dangerous way ever. I do, though, take your point about the risk of refusal to 'co-operate'. If that happens, we have no other options. I fully understand your position, Phil, but… this is too important; this is a one-shot opportunity that we can't pass up on. Bob? Neil?"

There was a momentary pause, and finally, Bob, sweeping his gaze around the expectant faces said: "I have to leave the moral decisions to you, I'm afraid, but I do understand the dilemma, and Phil's discomfort. Could I ask how we 'leak' this information without it setting off alarm bells within the IRA? Your man has been below the radar for 20 years, why would he surface now?" He swept a look across the faces, looking for reaction, ideas or encouragement, and saw none. Phil exchanged even more uncomfortable looks with Mike.

"The simple answer to that is we don't know yet, and in truth, we don't even know where Sam is, or even if he is still alive" Phil said. "I guess we need your help with that, Neil, 'cos we think he used to live in your patch. Mike has a phone number for him, but hasn't used it for a while."

"I agree with Bob." Neil Maynard had everyone's attention. "You guys have to decide how to approach it with your man, or not, as the case may be. It's fraught with all sorts of problems and risks, and not just for your 'tethered goat'. If this goes wrong, and we all know what 'going wrong' can mean, we are stuffed with a capital F. So, I'm not happy, but... I have high-level instructions to provide whatever resource, co-operation or assistance you require. Give me what you have on Sam's 'last known', and we'll find him. What you do then is up to you, I guess."

"Actually, it's not", George said, looking at Dave Rogers. "This is now an SIS fronted op. It's up to Dave to tell us how he wants this to proceed." All eyes were now on the so far silent 'spook', who was absorbing and assimilating all the information. He was clearly calculating risk, running scenarios, modelling chain of events, outcomes and assessing the abilities of this hastily assembled team. He looked at the expectant faces, held eye contact with George, and then Stuart-Rea, who looked down at his notes, moved on to Phil, who looked toward George, and finally, looked toward Mike. Mike held unwavering eye contact, and Dave 'Dodge' Rogers stood.

"If I've got this right, it was you who had the relationship with Sam, Mike?"

"Yes." Mike replied, "We were buddied up for a while, but Phil knew him well because he trained Sam in survival and evasion stuff. It's been a few years since we last hooked up, and, if I remember correctly, he was living in Cheshire, worked in transport, logistics, warehouses, that sort of thing. I used to call him when

I was back home, and, because he travelled around a lot with his job, we'd meet up at a pub somewhere and get pissed, on his expenses. Last time it was in South London 'cos I was flying out of Heathrow the day after, back to the sun and sand, again."

"Can I go back to Bob's original question – how are you suggesting we 'leak' this to the IRA?"

"Phil has contacts with local IRA men through UK Trade and Investments", Mike said, "Phil manages a group of undercover Field Officers in Belfast who have infiltrated at least two IRA Battalions; my idea is that we drop it into them. We know that there has always been an interest in tracking down Speccy Five Eyes; it can easily be an unguarded moment in the pub, said to the wrong person, or the right person – if you prefer."

"Is that achievable, Phil?" There was a long pause.

Phil gave Mike a long stare, turned to face Dave, and said: "Feasible, possible, risky, all sorts of issues but, yes, we could do it, if we think of the right channel."

There was another pause. Dave was clearly thinking through the strategy; individual roles, responsibilities and, inevitably, the down sides and repercussions of failure. He took a deep breath, looked at the expectant faces and said: "Right then! George is point man for all comms and will disseminate info to us all."

Looking for agreement from George, who nodded, Dave continued: "Neil and his guys will locate Sam", a nod from Neil, "and Mike will be the lead on surveillance and protection, with support from Neil's guys. Phil will look after the flow of info across the water, with any help he needs from Bob. Questions then?" There were none, each with his own thoughts. "Okay, then.

Let George know when you have found Sam, Neil, and we'll take it from there. Time is critical here, but let's get everything right before we move. George, keep us all up to speed, but if you think we need a meet, shout. I have to get back to London, and I'm sure you all have stuff you need to get to." He gathered his files and left the room, followed by Neil.

Bob hesitated, nodded at the army lads, and then said: "Perhaps we can have five minutes before I leave, Phil; I could do with chatting through how you want to set this up in Belfast, and what involvement you want from me, if any." There was a hint of sarcasm, which was not lost by the three.

"Sure, just give me a minute with George, and I'll catch you up.

As the door closed, Mike said, with a grin: "Guess who thinks he should be running the show then."

"Understandable," George said, "It all started in his patch, and I can see why he would want to front it. You'll have to be diplomatic with him, Phil; try not to upset him more than you have to, this may end up in his backyard again."

"I'll be gentle with him, but I need to talk to you both about this strategy; exposing Sam like this makes me very uncomfortable. It's not just Sam, he's probably got a wife and extended family. We are going to be stretched to say the least, to cover them all."

"Let's wait and see what Maynard comes up with, and then we can have another meet and sort out the protection issues. Just remember, the word is "whatever it takes", and "no stone unturned", and that's direct from the PM's Office, Phil. Look, I know you are unhappy about this, but that is the decision we have made, and I expect you to accept that. I know you will put your misgivings aside, and sort things for us at your end."

George, standing, signalled the end of conversation. Further discussion, disagreement or objection was pointless, and Phil knew he had lost – and knew when to keep his mouth shut. They all left the conference room without further comment or pleasantries, each lost in their own thoughts.

Chapter 28

May 1998

Phil sat in his office chair and pondered: how do I get this message "out there" in a credible way, without it obviously being deliberately leaked? He thought about the previous few days, and the different conversations that he had been party to. He profoundly disagreed with what had been agreed but... he was tasked with achieving a result, and what he thought about the ethics of it were irrelevant. He had a job to do. He had been churning it over all day. It was after eight, the office was quiet, only the night duty staff were in the office.

He left his office and threaded his way between the desks towards the coffee machine, deep in thought. Headphone wearing heads nodded greetings as he passed, but without verbal exchanges. All the ops lads were engrossed in monitoring radio mics, listening to bugs, and monitored phone lines. He leaned against the wall, waiting for the cup to fill and surveyed the room, hoping for inspiration. He had a meeting arranged with Bob Litt at eight in the morning, and was expected to put a credible plan on the table. Just ring a snout and tell him? Just chuck a file on a pub table and walk away? Offer it for sale? Put an ad in the paper? Nothing grabbed him; he was comprehensively uninspired.

He dumped three big spoonfuls of sugar into the black coffee, stirred, ran a hand through his thinning hair, and trudged wearily back to his office. He stopped half way, turned into the computer room, grabbed an empty office chair and pushed it, one handed, to Sheila's desk. Sheila Brooks, without an 'e' (she always said they couldn't afford the 'e'), was one of the cyber geeks that monitored the department's database. Her role in the department was not just to protect it from hackers, but to identify them, and determine who they were and why they were 'interested' in their data. Sheila was also the target of much attention from most male colleagues, who were not just trying to get into her intellect. She always seemed to be unaware of how attractive she was, sort of unobtainable, but available at the same time. Somehow, she was able to turn a business suit into a basque. She smiled, as Phil slumped into the chair

"I'd ask if this was social, an invite to dinner, drinks or picnic by the river, but to be honest, you look shit, Phil, so I guess it's business?"

"Maybe I'll give you a ring when Angela has gone to her mother's for the weekend, but no, it's not social." He turned the chair side-on, put the coffee on her desk, and put his hands behind his head. Gazing at the ceiling, he paused, in thought; she waited.

"Tell me, how easy would it be to allow a hacker to access a file without compromising other files that we don't want him to see?"

"Well, it doesn't work like that, I'm afraid. If you get in, you're in; you can access everything in all the files that are in the database you have accessed. I guess that is not the answer that you wanted, so why don't you just tell me what it is that you really want, if it's not me."

"Well, I want to give the bad guys some info without them knowing that we have done it deliberately. Because we know they are constantly trying to hack into our system, I wondered if we could allow them to get in, but stop them from seeing stuff we don't want them to see." He paused, "I can see from your face that I'm not explaining this too well."

"No! It's ok, I've got it, but there is a simpler way, which is to do it through an email account. If we fill it with meaningless crap, include the info you want leaked, we then just use an insecure password that they have managed to access before, one that is already compromised. Simple really." She smiled. Phil was stunned at the simplicity of it.

"Can you set it up for me then, and then give me the email address, and I'll get someone to email it with the info I want to leak?"

"Sure, but it will take a day or so, and it will cost you." Another smile and she continued, "But you can pay me 'in kind', if you like." Phil smiled, and, with a wink, acknowledging the obvious invitation, left the office with a new spring in his step, like a weight had been lifted. Back in his own office, he pulled Neil Maynard's card from his file and dialled the number, not expecting to get an answer at this time in the evening. He was surprised when it was answered abruptly.

"Maynard?"

"Oh, er, hello Neil, it's Phil, UKTI. Didn't expect you to still be there at this time of night, and was just going to leave a message. Have you made any progress?"

"Well, actually, yes we have. We've got an address for our man, and as you guys suspected, he is still local to us – lives with his wife in a nice quiet area, nothing on the radar about him at all. We've not done anything with it yet – wanted to see how you wanted to progress things."

"Well, we've got a plan to get the info 'out there', but will probably not be ready until tomorrow, so I'll let you know as soon as I can. The plan is to get you to email me our man's name and address to a specific email account. The down side is that this will probably mean that the email address you send it from will also become vulnerable, so you may want to put in your own security stuff before you send anything."

"OK Phil, understood. Thanks for the call."

Neil put the phone down, stared at it: 'That's obvious', he thought, 'so what the hell did you ring me for, then?'

Phil put the phone down, and said to himself: 'That's obvious, what the hell did I ring him for?'

He answered his own question in his head; he wanted to share the breakthrough about the planed leak, as it had been troubling him so much. 'I'm getting too old for this', he thought, 'Why do I feel the need to seek approval for the strategy from Mr Plod; I think it's time I gave up'. He paused, 'The reality is that we are all old now, Me, Mike OB, George, Sam and Billy One. I wonder if we are actually too old? Can we really do this anymore?'

Sheila woke him just before midnight with coffee, a disgusting sticky bun with currents in, icing on the top and a proud announcement that she had built an email account with a credible history, pasted from previous insignificant accounts. She was confident that it would appear legitimate, that it could, and would, be hacked and that, at the time of creation, contained nothing of value to any 'intruder'. Sheila was clearly 'buzzing', really pleased with what she had achieved in such a short space of time. Neil was slightly uncomfortable with thanking her for her efforts and hard work too profusely, without putting himself in a position that led to 'other things'. He was, however, truly grateful, appreciative and impressed. He could see that if he was not very careful, he could succumb to the charms and delights of an IT wizard (or witch).

Iced sticky bun and coffee revived him; he felt almost human.

He went home.

Chapter 29

May 1998

Phil churned it over all night. He felt as if he had not slept at all, but forced himself out of bed and into the real world. He sat in the kitchen at the breakfast bar, elbows on the worktop, waiting for the toast to pop. It did, and along with it came the decision that had eluded him all night. He felt better already, buttering the toast, gulping coffee, arms into jacket sleeves, passing toast from hand to hand; he left the flat, eating on the move. The drive to the office was rehearsal time, and he talked to himself and the rear-view mirror.

He negotiated the desks, office detritus and "good mornings" and, unusually for him, walked straight to his office, back heeling the door closed and went for the phone. Two rings and without preamble, Phil said: "Can you talk, Mike?"

"Err, yeah, just give me a minute." There were muffled voices; a hand over the phone moment, rustling and Mike was back: "What's up, mate?"

"I'm not going to go over it all again, Mike, I understand your feelings, but I want to give Sam a very discrete heads-up without going against the decision that was taken."

"Risky Phil. Apart from going up against George and the others, Stewart-Rae will remove your bollocks if Sam refuses at the first fence."

"Fully aware of that, but I have a plan to make sure Sam is not given an option. But, if he is totally unaware that he has been targeted, he's a little tin duck in the IRA shooting gallery."

"OK, let's say for a minute that I agree with you, what exactly are you asking me?"

"Well, I need some way of letting him know without anyone realising it, some sort of code if you like. Something that only us and Sam would recognise." There was silence.

After a good twenty seconds: "Are you still there, Mike?"

"Yeah, I'm here. You'll have to let me think about this, Phil. My first thought is that it would have to be non-attributable, to keep you clean, but not so obscure that it's not recognisable by Sam. It has to be something from the past that he will instantly see as an IRA link. Maybe a link to 'Derry? But that's not really going to give him the message, is it? If it's going to work, it should be a link to Billy One, that's the only way you are going to..."

Mike's voice trailed off, back into silent thought.

"Go on Mike, what are you thinking?" There was another pause.

"Something we laughed about a lot, sort of black humour really – but he would remember it for sure, and he would instantly link it to Billy Conlan."

"Go on."

"Well, we were at the inquest into Billy's mother's death; Sam was a witness, but wasn't identified – he was just referred to as 'soldier B', but everyone knew him by his street name of Speccy Five Eyes. I was there as his

Minder. Sam was called, and he gave evidence about the photographs that led to Billy's mums arrest, but we talked during recesses, as much to ease the boredom as anything. He related this story of the riot, funny really; I can remember it all clearly. He said it was at the junction of Sackville Street, and I think Little James Street; he said he was in a shop doorway, with his knees knocking, when Billy's mum stood out in the open, on her own, facing fifty tooled up Squaddies, chucking cups and saucers from a cardboard box at them. I don't know if that's any use to you, but Sam would certainly remember it."

"Not sure how I can use that, Mike, but it's the sort of thing I'm after. I'll have a think, but if you come up with anything else let me know. Where are you by the way?"

"I'm in Cheshire in the Ops room, well, in the corridor outside it, actually."

The phone call ended, and Phil sat looking at the phone for several minutes, deep in thought. He needed to get Neil Maynard on side with his plan, but could see how easily this could go tits up. If his judgement of Maynard was right... well, it would have to be right. That was his next phone call.

"Maynard".

"Neil, I could do with meeting up. Can we sort something out, say, tomorrow?"

"Oh! Hi Phil, how are you? What's your weather like? How's the family?"

The sarcasm was not lost on Phil. "Sorry, Neil, I'm a bit stressed, but I really do need to talk some stuff through with you urgently, and not over the phone. If I nip over tomorrow, is there any chance you could meet me?"

"Not a problem, except that I have a two hour-ish briefing that I can't duck at eight in the morning, and I have a family thing at seven in the evening – and it would start the third world war if you make me miss it."

"Great, thanks Neil. I'll email you with when and where when I've sorted stuff out, but will try and make it mid-day-ish."

His next call was to George Bennett, who didn't hesitate or question why Phil had an urgent need to meet with Maynard. He accepted that Phil knew what he was doing, and arranged a taxi for him from Belfast heliport to Barton Aerodrome on the outskirts of Manchester. He agreed that the Lynx would wait and take him home again, as long as Phil committed to a stay no longer than two hours on the ground. Departure was agreed at 10:00 which, with a flight distance of 180 miles, the Lynx would do it in an hour or so.

He emailed Neil: "*Barton Aerodrome (assume you know where that is) eta 11:30-ish, you choose lunch venue, I'll pay. Must leave by 2 so don't blame any subsequent family war on me.*"

As they approached, Phil looked through the small window at the Manchester Ship Canal, then at the nearly completed Trafford Centre – little toy sized cars packed into spaces too small. As they descended, getting closer to warehouse roofs, dust and leaves obscured his view, and his gaze reverted to the sparse interior of his taxi. They landed with a jolt, and looking out of the now open door, Phil could see some distance away, the approaching vehicle. A little bit wind-swept and cold, Phil was pleased to get into the warm and quiet comfort of Neil's Range Rover. It was an unmarked 'ballistically protected' covert, Armed Response Vehicle (ARV). It was driven by an equally, unmarked and covert, incommunicative driver, presumably also armed, possibly also with protected ballisticals. Hands were shaken in the back seats, and they swept out of the Aerodrome two miles up the road to The Unicorn, a nondescript, seen better days pub. All three walked into the pub, to be greeted by the smell of stale beer, a thousand fags, and a welcoming, smiling, cleavage.

Phil took the lead with: "What would you like, chaps?"

"Can I have a coke please, in the bottle, not a glass, and a bag of cheese and onion?" the driver asked.

"Neil?"

"I'll have a half of bitter and a ploughman's, please, Phil."

"And I'll have a large shiraz and two pork pies with some English mustard please, if you have it?"

"And where will you be sitting, gentlemen?"

It seemed a bit of a daft question, seeing as the place was empty, but going with it, Neil said: "We'll take the table in the corner by the window, if that's ok?", looking for approval or otherwise from Phil, who nodded his agreement and moved in the general direction of the designated table. Neil followed with his bitter, and Phil's Shiraz.

Coke, crisps and driver left to ensure the safety of the bullet proof ARV. Phil and Neil settled into the corner where they were able to talk uninhibited. After a pause for breath, a quick slurp, and, conscious that Neil was waiting for an explanation, Phil started with: "I'm really uncomfortable with…" only to be interrupted by the arrival of a ploughman's, his pork pies, and the requested mustard. Neil waited until the cleavage, and associated generous rump, departed.

"So, what exactly are you uncomfortable with, then?"

"You know that all of this started with Mike suggesting that we 'use' Sam as a tethered goat to get Billy One out in the open. I fully understand the tactical logic behind that, but I have a problem with exposing Sam, or anyone he is associated with in this way. Having worked with him for a while makes it even worse; I have a connection with him that I can't just ignore. It's difficult to explain, Neil, but, in the regiment, we have a responsibility to, and for, each other that transcends almost all other considerations. I worked with Sam; we shared stuff that most people wouldn't understand. I know that he was not like us, he wasn't a hard arse, he didn't knowingly, voluntarily, jump into this. He was totally out of his depth. We exposed him to stuff that he didn't sign up for, we put him in a position that he couldn't say no to.

We, on the other hand, knew exactly what we were signing up to. So, because of all that crap, I feel very guilty doing this to him, I have a duty, no, a responsibility, to do what I can to protect him, as much as I can. I've got a plan that I think works, but it needs your buy-in to make it work, and then makes it possible for me to sleep at night when this turns to rat shit. You said to me on the phone that Sam is living with his wife, and that's the first problem. We have got to get her away from this before we dangle the bait and expose Sam. Looking after him is one thing… looking after his family as well, is a completely different thing."

"We'll keep Sam very close, Phil. Mike will be 'close protection' lead; he knows Sam best, and will be trusted by Sam if we have to come out of the bushes."

Phil interrupted. "I agree with that, but we have to make sure everyone else is kept well away from this; if it goes wrong, and we have injuries to total innocents, we are going to be crucified, and you'll see the Westminster Suits running over the horizon to distance themselves from us. Ok! So, we need to clear the decks before we leak Sam's address. Get his misses out of there; get her to visit her mother in Australia for a month, that would be good."

Neil, who had been eating as he listened, speared a pickled gherkin with his fork, and, waving it towards Phil, said: "We'll get her out and stash her somewhere safe, but what do you suggest she tells Sam? She can't just disappear without telling him something. This is getting very difficult to manage, Phil. You still haven't told me what your plan is; I understand that you are 'uncomfortable' with it. So am I, for Christ's sake."

"I want to make sure that Sam knows that Billy One is coming for him, Neil. I get that we need to set him up, but we can't just leave him defenceless; we can protect him better if he knows who he's up against, otherwise, he will be exposed every step of the way and, yes, we'll get Billy, but we'll lose Sam, and I can't just do nothing to try and stop that."

"We have already agreed that we can't ask for Sam's help, and run the risk of him refusing; that was agreed at a very high level, Phil, and to go against that is career suicide for me."

"Yes, I know, so what I want to do is give Sam a message that only he will understand, and will not be recognised by our masters."

"And you can do that, can you?"

"No Neil, I can't – but you can, and you don't even need to know what the message is. I just need you to trust me and run with it." Neil made a great pretence of mopping up the remnants of his ploughman's, whilst he thought about a response.

"It's not going to be attributable, Neil; it won't be logged or recorded, so, here's the plan, but at this stage, without the timings."

Phil outlined everything, including the wording of the email exchange, and, back on board the Lynx, thought through everything. He was sweating and tense with the beginnings of a headache – pain up the back of his neck. 'I really am getting too old for this; I'd rather be playing golf.'

It was nearly 4 o'clock when they landed in Belfast, and it was still raining. As he walked away from the pad, collar up, shoulders hunched, he, again, felt the pain up the back of his neck, and tried to relax his shoulders. He felt a trickle of cold rain water run down his back and shivered. It took 20 minutes to get back to the office through the late afternoon traffic, as shoppers began to drift home along with the early office finishers – all trying to be ahead of the rush hour – turning it into 'rush 2 hours'.

"We've had a hit on the new email already." Sheila said with pride, as he shook rain off his coat and hung it all over the hat stand in the corner of his office.

"Great Sheila, let's get the first one out to Maynard, then."

Subject: Location request.

As discussed last week, our local Coroner's Office have asked if we can locate Soldier "B" who was a witness at the Inquest into the death of Maureen Conlan in 1971. All known info about him is in the file that I left with you, including his Military Service Record. This appears to be gathering momentum and I would be grateful if this could be treated as urgent.

Regards

P

Phil knew that Neil could respond immediately, but wanted to let a little time pass before the response came, so he rang Neil and suggested that he replied, as agreed, the following morning. He sat back in his chair, looked at the ceiling, and thought about asking Sheila to come and massage his neck; pleasant as that would be, he decided he'd better go home.

Chapter 30

May 1998

The email reply came in, as did Sheila, waving the hard copy triumphantly.

Subject: Location request.

We have the location requested with all current status info and report – see attachment. Please let me know if you need anything further and/or if you wish me to brief Mr Burgess and advise him that he may be required to attend a re-convened Coroner's Court.

Regards

N

P.S., Still waiting for that Golf invite.

"Have you got a copy of the attachment as well, Sheila?"

"Sure", she said, passing the second sheet to Phil.

"And will they have picked up the email and the attachment? How do we know they have it all? I'm sorry, I'm not doubting you, but I just need to know that this is actually doing what I need it to do. Sorry to be pushy, but my knob is on the block here, Sheila; it's really important."

"Yes, I can tell. I'm positive that this email has been hacked; I don't know yet who by, but I think it's by a site that we have seen before, and can attribute it to our friends. We'll have a better idea when we have tracked the IP address, but all we definitely know at this stage, is that this hacker is in our local area. I'm confident that it's the same site that accessed our site last month, and we know that that was a local IRA cell, because it led to them identifying our guy in Newry, and we had to pull him out quickly."

"Okay, send the next email, and let me know what you find about the hacking. Is there any danger that they would know that we know, if you see what I mean?"

"Yes, I understand, and no, they would not know that we know. I'll get on it."

Subject: Location request.

Thanks for that, Neil. No need to do anything yet. Just waiting for a decision from the Court. Suspect that they are waiting for more info before proceeding or not but at least we are ready if they do decide to proceed. No point in contacting Mr Burgess yet and unsettling him. If you could just keep track of him in the interim so we can get hold of him quickly if we need to. Clearly, because of the sensitivity of all of this 'locally' he (Mr Burgess) will need to be looked after, there are concerns about his safety if his whereabouts is disclosed to our friends.

Not forgotten about our golf challenge.

Thanks again for your help.

P

There was nothing he could do now other than wait. He was sort of elated, but controlled. He couldn't get the thought out of his mind that he was fundamentally responsible for putting his ex-colleague in serious danger, and knew that he would have trouble dealing with the guilt if this went wrong. With a deep breath, he turned his attention to the pile of correspondence on the desk that he had neglected for the past week.

Chapter 31

May 1998

The Liverpool city bar wasn't exactly crowded for a Friday night, but it was buzzing; loud throbbing music pounded in his chest. It was considered to be 'the place to be' in the early evening by the wealthy from the local business and commercial community. Complimentary olives and peanuts in dishes on the bar, cocktails, if you wanted them, and serious bullshit, like it or not.

Some had clearly been in the bar since leaving desks and offices at five, and now, at eight, were probably not going to be still standing at nine. He was there to hunt out a vulnerable woman who he could entertain for a while in the hope that she would reciprocate. He considered this to be his 'local', a frequent hunting ground.

She had chosen a barstool and positioned herself so that anyone coming into the bar would see legs and cleavage first, bar tenders and staff second. She was at her best, looking delicious, sultry, discrete, but at the same time, obviously available, a candle flame to a moth.

Luke was no exception – a moth, and, although his objective was to order a drink, given that there were several other places at the bar, it was much more inviting to order whilst standing next to the tanned, stunning, and obviously alone lady, rather than to squeeze into the throng at the end of the bar where all the bar staff were.

"Can I have a pint of Fosters, please?" He shouted to try and make himself heard above the sound of the music, and everyone else who was also shouting to make themselves heard.

"What"? Was the reply from the guy with a ring in his ear, which obviously detracted from his hearing ability.

"Fosters. Pint", Luke yelled.

"Sorry, mate. What?"

"Pint. Fosters" Luke shouted. The lady intervened and interpreted on Luke's behalf; it was clearly an issue of pitch, rather than volume. With a nod of understanding, the bar man smiled and poured.

"Thanks for the intervention," Luke said, leaning closer than was necessary to make himself heard.

"No problem." The stunning lady replied with a melting smile. There was an uncomfortable exchange of smiles, nods and a feeble but prolonged attempt at conversation on Luke's behalf, which, with many gestures, he established that the lady would, "Yes please", like another Chenin Blanc.

After drinks were drunk, shouts were shouted, and gesticulations were gesticulated. "This is hopeless," she said "We can't talk in here, would you like to go to the Pub next door? I'm Bridget, who are you?"

"Yes, let's do it, I'm Luke. Would you like to hear my life story, Bridget?"

The cold air had a sobering effect, and Luke couldn't quite believe that he had pulled so easily, but, 'what the hell', she was hot.

The 'Bull' was much more civilised, and conversation far easier. Bridget explained that she was in Liverpool for a meeting the next day with representatives from a soft drinks company that she was hoping to agree a vending supply contract with. She was happily divorced, unattached, on her own, in a city that was unfamiliar, and was pleased to have met such an amiable, happy scouser.

"I'm not a scouser!" Luke exclaimed in mock outrage, "I'm Irish, and proud of it".

"So, tell me your life story then, Luke."

"Born and dragged up in Belfast, left in '82 came to Liverpool, and started my own business, and I've got three garages now around the city, doing servicing, MOTs and insurance repairs."

They left the pub at ten, and she staggered, and needed support as the fresh air hit. "You ok?" Luke asked, pulling her close to him, purely to support her, of course, but it was enjoyable.

She looked up at him. "Thank you. You are a gentleman aren't you, Luke." She leaned into him, and kissed him hard. "I'm staying at the Travelodge; do you want to come back with me? I'm not usually this forward, but I really like you, and well, life's too short, so take me to bed."

"Can I think about it? – OK, I've thought about it." He pushed her against the wall and they kissed again, this time with tongues, moans, panting, urgency and thrusting.

"No, stop, take me to bed." She said.

The passion increased in the lift, they paused three times in the long corridor for more fondling and groping, giggling like school kids when they were interrupted en-route by another resident, who smiled approvingly as he passed them 'mid clinch'. She pushed Luke away, and fumbled for the key card, took two goes at inserting the card, and then fell, stumbling, through the door, with Luke in hot pursuit.

He grabbed her from behind, cupping her breasts and rubbing his erection against her bottom, and she bent forward pushing back in response. They staggered towards the bed and fell together, laughing, across the bed. She disentangled herself from his grasp and panting, breathless, kissed his ear and whispered, "Just a minute, I need the bathroom, get undressed and into bed and I'll be back in a minute." She wiggled provocatively, looking over her shoulder, smiling and disappeared into the bathroom.

He undressed, sat on the end of the bed and considered how to pose for best effect for her return. He reclined, decided he didn't look good, he stood, no that didn't look good either, moved pillows, lay back with one leg raised so that she would see his erection first, and then decided he should take his socks off too.

In the bathroom, Bridget washed her face and hands, took a deep breath and composed herself. She sat on the toilet seat, retrieved her phone from her bag, pressed send on the already input text message, and waited for a reply. Her phone pinged as the text reply arrived; she counted to twenty and left the bathroom. As she came out, she glanced at Luke, who was grinning at her, lying on the bed slowly rubbing his erection in an attempt to stave off the effects of five pints of Fosters. She smiled, "Hang on to that for a minute," and she walked to the door, opening it to admit Nick.

Luke was confused, but his focus was on the silenced pistol now pointed at what used to be an erection. All thoughts of rampant sex gone, he made a feeble attempt to cover his modesty with the sheets as if they would deflect 9mm of instant contraception.

They sat on either side of the bed. Luke was rapidly sobering up, wondering what the hell was happening to him. Who was she, who was he, what was happening, what was going to happen? An elbow on his chest and the muzzle of the pistol was pushed into his mouth, cold metallic taste and pain, as it was pushed against the back of his throat. He was rigid with fear, all thoughts of sex now abandoned.

The sheets were stripped from him, vulnerable, totally exposed. Although he couldn't see past the arm on his chest, the gun and the face of the man holding it, he felt the ties pulling his ankle bones painfully together, followed by his wrists being equally secured. He felt the needle go into his thigh.

"Not a fucking sound, or you're dead – your choice." The gun was removed from his mouth, only to be replaced by his own underpants. It was at this point that he lost control of bladder and bowel functions. The injection had begun to take effect, and he lost the ability to move his arms and legs.

"We are here to show you what happens when you take money that doesn't belong to you; Aedan Carney sends his regards." He didn't know what the injection was, but he knew it would not be a painkiller.

Winnie smiled: "Wait, Nick. I owe this bastard after what I have had to do." Luke felt the shock of ice-cold liquid on his genitals. He struggled to free himself and to fight, but his legs wouldn't work, and being tied, with Nick's weight on his chest, he was unable to move. He heard the clicking of the cigarette lighter, and then smelt the burning before he felt the pain, as his pubic hair ignited; the liquid had concentrated in a pool under his scrotum – he screamed, as his testicles were flambéed, the unheard scream in his head and his underpants.

Winnie and Nick were getting out of the lift as the fire alarm started. People were drifting outside, staff were shrugging with confused unconcern.

"It'll be a false alarm, but could you all assemble in the car park across the street, please." Said a suited receptionist. Winnie and Nick split up as they left the reception area, stepping out into the cool evening air. Mingling with the assembled evacuees and the curious passers-by, Nick keyed a number into his phone and waited.

In a Londonderry betting shop, the nasal gruff Ulster voice of Aedan Carney said: "Is it done?"

"Yes", Nick said, "but I need an hour before you go public."

"Only an hour then; I need to get the message out there that you don't rip-off our funds and fuck with the IRA. I have a present for you though, Nick. Just to show you how grateful I am, I know where an old friend of yours is, Speccy Five Eyes."

Nick stopped in his tracks: "Where?"

"Tomorrow, Nick." The call was ended, and Nick glanced at Winnie, nodded and turned away, threading his way through the crowd. Flames could now be seen on the third floor, sirens could be heard as the police and fire engines fought their way through the traffic.

They met up again outside Debenhams, linked arms and appeared to look with interest at the shop window display but, in reality, just the reflection of the activity outside the City Hotel.

The next morning, the media reports were all about the murder of a garage proprietor, and small-time gangster with known IRA connections, in a Liverpool hotel. A short statement from the IRA confirmed that they had carried out the assassination, claiming that the dead man had "misappropriated" IRA funds, and this was the punishment that should be expected.

Nick waited as long as he could, and, finally, next morning, gave in, and stopped between deliveries to ring. Without preamble, Aedan gave him the name and address he wanted. Nick immediately started planning and considering the options; he now finally, knew the name of Speccy Five Eyes, and the address where he lived.

Struck by the attitude of his IRA Master, it was just assumed by them that he would carry on doing their bidding forever. But, even they didn't know his identity; he was just a phone number and a guy called Nick. It was at this point that Nick first started to think about his own exit strategy and his retirement. Speccy Five Eyes was to be the last.

Chapter 32

May 1998

It had been a month since the last big job, which had not been a problem, but Nick had begun to become a bit anxious about what the next job was going to be, and when it was going to appear. He had been lucky; so far, he was still below the radar. He was still unknown, unidentified and anonymous. He was realistic though; he knew that his luck would run out one day soon. He was also concerned that Winnie might be identified on hotel CCTV as the woman in the Liverpool bar who had been seen with the late Luke Brennan.

There was a tension between him and Winnie, which was understandable, given their life style. Nick was a realist; he knew how careful they had to be, how he was reliant upon Aedan Carney, and was aware that his safety was dependent upon the integrity of the Irish network. Nick constantly played the 'what if' scenarios in his head. If it came to the 'end game', he knew Winnie would save herself if she could, even if it meant selling him out, shopping him, or even worse (he couldn't quite bring himself to think it through). He had seen her kill, seen her set fire to people, and seen her smile. He knew that she had actually enjoyed the power, the control, inflicting pain and suffering. He, on the other had had a mission, a calling, a job to do and enjoyment or satisfaction didn't feature at all. Her 'dark side' worried him, and he knew that, one day, they would need to confront it. They had a strange, but mutually dependent love, that they both realised could never be found with any other.

He had, after long deliberations, decided to sever the connections with his past life. He had one more job to do, and then would have avenged his family and repaid the debt to Joe Murphy and Aedan Carney. He had served 'the cause' well – done a good job. He was still only a phone number to everyone across the water. He had 'disappeared' before, and could do it again. His biggest concern was the lock-up garage with its incriminating contents, and how to dispose of his 'soon to be surplus' stock. Now, with the information about the identity of Speccy Five Eyes and his location, he had a new focus and a plan. The irony of it made him smile. This, for Nick, was his 'end game'.

The Transit van he had bought at the auction was a real wreck – serious engine problems; it had a very loud engine knock and rattle that suggested a limited life. It cost a fortune to run, almost using as much oil as diesel, requiring oil every 100 miles or so. The cab filled with fumes as it rattled along, and they had to keep the windows open as they drove to avoid passing out. Aldershot town centre on a Saturday evening was no place to leave a van unattended for long before it attracted attention, but with a driver in it, it was just another late evening delivery.

"Pull over here, and stop outside the shop". The shop was a 9 'till 11 convenience store, squashed between a pub and an Italian restaurant. Nick looked at his watch again, running through the timings, calculating the time he needed, he waited, eyes flitting from Winnie, to wrist watch, to pedestrians, to traffic and back to his watch. Time to go and he put on his hi-vis yellow vest.

"I need you to stay with the van while I go and have a look at the target" Nick said. "I'll only be ten minutes, and then we can get going."

Earlier, he had suggested that they do this job and take the opportunity to have a night together in London, have a nice romantic meal, see a show – whatever she fancied doing – a leisurely breakfast, then get the train back to Manchester.

"I'm taking our bag, so I don't look out of place. Put the hazards on, and look like you're on the phone. I'm going to open the back doors, so it looks like we're doing a delivery. If anyone shows any interest, just say that I'm delivering to the shop. I'll be back in a few minutes." Nick jumped out, slung the bag over his shoulder, and walked to the back of the van. He opened both the rear doors, which revealed six large bulk boxes of Crisps: three wide, two high, obscuring any other contents.

The shop was empty; the grumpy lad behind the counter didn't look up from his phone. It had been a long day, business was bad, no one was buying much tonight, just the odd packet of fags or breath-fresheners bought by people starting out on a big night out. He wished he too was on a big night out, didn't want to 'be here'. He didn't notice Nick remove his yellow vest and stuff it into the sack that had been slung over his shoulder. His phone chimed to signify a reply to his last text, but he didn't read it because he had a customer at last. Nick pushed the sandwich pack and bottle of water towards him with a smile; they were scanned:

"Two sixty please, mate", he said.

Nick, momentarily, thought about complaining about the exorbitant price, gave him three quid, smiled and said, "Keep it, mate. Ta!" Smiling, Nick stuffed the carton and bottle into his sack bag, pulled the ties on the bag, slung it back over his shoulder, and left the shop.

As Nick left the shop, he glanced at the van, rear doors still open, hazard lights flashing. Couples arm in arm were walking round it, laughing, and enjoying the evening. Tight T-Shirts, emphasising muscles, with even tighter trousers. Short skirts and skimpy tops, exposing buttocks and breasts. He paused, momentarily; the Italian was beginning to fill, the window tables crowded, some customers eating, some drinking, and some waiting for food to arrive. He could smell the garlic – feel the warmth and the ambiance, the obvious enjoyment of these lovely people having a really good night out.

He stepped off the pavement to allow a couple that were walking, arms around each other, to pass into oblivion. There was a duo playing Bob Dylan covers in the Pub, three at the door smoking, tapping feet and engaging with passers-by. He turned the corner, picked up his pace and hailed a taxi.

A few minutes later, the taxi stopped at the Railway Station, he hesitated, unsure momentarily that he was doing the right thing; he got out, paid, and walked onto the London bound platform. It had taken no more than eight minutes, and he had two more minutes before the train departed for London. He waited, phone in hand and then got onto the train. The doors closed, platform announcements were made, and the train slowly jerked forward, and, as it started to move, he made the call.

Winnie didn't get a phone call; neither did she hear the sound. She didn't feel the intense heat. She didn't feel it when her head penetrated the van roof; she didn't feel it when her charred body, clothing burned completely, hit the second floor of the restaurant, or when it then descended into what remained of the kitchen which was on fire. She was subsequently designated as being an "un-identified customer" in the restaurant (without a yellow vest). An almost intact beer pump handle was found to be embedded in the chest of an eighteen-year old student, a pub customer. The twenty-two-year-old fireman who found her would never admit to his colleagues that he had removed his respirator to vomit, as he worked with them to extract the girl's body, and then help to retrieve the other thirty two bodies.

Chapter 33

11th June 1998

Back in Devizes, at the end of October 1969, I had started demob leave, and set about finding a job. I spent a few years aimlessly "wandering" in terms of jobs, eventually, over the years, finding my niche in road transport – controlling trucks, managing warehouses and distribution contracts. Starting in planning and traffic control, I moved to contract management, which took me into business development. My last job was with a multi-depot distribution company, with a main depot in Cardiff. They had other depots all over the country, and ran a complicated network of night trunk vehicles, feeding a fleet of vans, which would deliver from the depots the next day.

I spent a lot of time on the road with customers in Aberdeen and Plymouth, and, I guess, this was a contributing factor in ending my marriage to Jane. Her complete disinterest in sexual activity did not excuse my 'affair', but I am still troubled by the blame that I bore rather than expose what went on (or didn't go on) behind closed doors – if you know what I mean.

I had missed the 'buzz' of army life, and tried to replace it, firstly as a passenger in the racing sidecar outfit that I helped build with Fred, and then by navigating a rally car that I built with Alan (my two brothers-in-law at the time). In the summers, I climbed on rock in Derbyshire and Wales. In the winters, I climbed on ice on the 'Ben' (Ben Nevis) in Aviemore with John D (another ex regiment man); days on 'The Ben', with nights in the Red McGregor – really good memories.

I was unable to replace what I had come to think was normality; there was an empty 'pointlessness' about everything that alcohol or adrenalin couldn't numb or replace. In retrospect, I had convinced myself that I was 'dealing with stuff'. In reality, I was screaming for help – no one knew where I had been or where I was going; certainly not me.

As things deteriorated in my marriage, it coincided with bowel cancer; fingers up my arse, blood tests, bag of spanners up my arse, more blood tests, major surgery, nothing up or down my arse, and a bag to collect 'stuff' in. A dark time, with very little to laugh about, but we always find humour somehow in these situations. Bored with lying in a hospital bed, the routine blood pressure, temperature checks and ECGs. I was surrounded by nurses to do yet another ECG, this time with a trainee who had never done it before.

"Make sure all the pads have a good contact with the skin, avoiding the hairy areas if you can, attach the electrodes, and switch the machine on." Nervous trainee nurse began sticking the pads all over me, and clipped in the electrodes, smiling unconfidently at me, as she pretended to know what she was doing.

"We are not going to hurt each other, are we?" I asked.

"Oh no," she said, "It won't hurt, I promise." she smiled.

Senior Nurse said: "OK, switch on and check connectivity" Clearly nothing was happening, so she switched off and checked all the connections. She switched on again, and, as she did so, I faked convulsions, jerking about on the bed as if electrocuted. "SWITCH IT OFF, SWITCH IT OFF!", shouted the nurse. It amused me, and helped alleviate the boredom.

Later, I was asked by the sadistic, 'experienced' nurse to repeat my 'performance' for the next 'trainee'. How could I possibly refuse?

More surgery, goodbye bag, hello normality and then Liver Cancer; more blood sucking, surgery again, more tests, more BP, more temperature checks, more ECGs, and yes, I did do the convulsions trick again. Chemo followed, then surgery again, and (touch wood), I was finally pronounced clear of the big 'C'. It was all over, along with my marriage – and it was June 1998.

Taking stock, I was single, reasonably fit and well now, and to my surprise, found that I had been 'retired', and could spend the rest of my life doing whatever I wanted to do. I had my little cottage in Cheshire, a garage that I could 'tinker' in with my spanners, a room upstairs that I could paint in (oil on canvas, not the bloody walls), I could cook for the many lady friends that would be queuing at my door, and I could build upon the extensive six bottle wine cellar that I had built up over many years (hours actually – from the supermarket). I could set about spending the rest of my life doing whatever I wanted to do.

It would be good when I decided what that was going to be, but, at the moment, survival seemed like a good plan, as long as Detective Inspector Maynard and Billy One would allow it.

Chapter 34

11th June 1998

I was still coming down from the adrenaline rush of playing burglar in what used to be my own back garden.

The unwrapped bundle was spread across the kitchen table. A Browning "Hi Power" Semi-Automatic 9mm pistol, 13 round magazine, and a box of 50, 9x19mm parabellum rounds. "Thanks, OB", I muttered, feeling the comfort of the 1kg weight, transferring it from hand to hand, smelling the oil. I pulled back the mechanism, cocking the weapon, and then pulled the trigger, holding back the recoil mechanism so that the firing pin was not damaged. I stripped and cleaned it, surprising myself with the ease and comfort I felt handling it after all these years. I filled the 13 round mag, and inserted it with a satisfying click, as it was located into the pistol grip.

I put the pistol into the back of my jeans, just like they do in the films, put the box in my fleece pocket, and the cloth it was wrapped in went into the bin under the sink.

Picking up my glass and the bottle, I went back into the living room thinking, 'I need some music, and to think things through.' Collecting the remote from the computer desk, I stood in front of the TV, flicked through the channels, found Vintage TV and joined an Eagles track. Putting the remote on the coffee table, retrieving the bottle from the computer desk, I crossed to the other side of the coffee table, and, as I bent to put the bottle down, my heart stopped, dead, I was frozen to the spot.

There was a dark patch on the carpet just in front of my 'telly-watching' armchair leg. It was the indentation in the carpet left by the leg; it had been moved, only by two inches, but moved. Someone had been in my house. But I had checked everywhere when I'd come in; the doors were locked, nothing had changed, no one was lurking in the back, all the rooms were empty – I'd even looked under the bed.

I switched the TV off, switched the lights off, and opened the curtains a crack. The black Audi was back. I stood for a moment, thinking about the Audi, and slowly let the curtains close, and put the lights and TV back on. I leaned back against the wall between the door and the window, and looked around the room. I thought about the implications of the chair being moved. There were only three chairs: my 'office' dining room chair, and my two easy chairs, one either side of the coffee table. It was obvious that one was for visitors, and one was for TV watching. There was a clear route through – no reason to move the chair. I moved the coffee table, revealed the four marks that the legs had created, and then replaced it in the same position. It clearly hadn't been moved, but it would have been far easier to move than the chair.

So, not moved because of some obstruction, moved for some other reason. I sat on the coffee table, elbows on knees, and studied the chair: 'Why were you moved?'

Looking around the room slowly and carefully, nothing else was out of place, nothing else had been moved. Back to the chair – it all seemed normal, but, something... The base cushion had sagged with constant use, and, looking over my shoulder at its twin, I saw similar signs of usage. It too had a saggy bottom, but not as bad as the TV chair. Looking back, though, and comparing the two, the TV chair didn't seem to be quite as saggy as it should have been.

And then it clicked; it was that moment of realisation, and I slowly stood, stepped carefully sideways away from the chair, and realised that I was shaking, sweaty, heart racing. I forced deep breaths, tried to calm myself, and then, very carefully, crawled on hands and knees to the front of the chair. There, at eye level with the bottom of the cushion, I could see that there was something under it that shouldn't have been there.

Sitting on the floor now, I tried to think through the options. Get out, walk away (no, run like fuck), just leave everything as it is, or investigate further and risk finding what I thought I was going to find – what to do?

I thought about what would happen if I left it. The fact was, I didn't really know what was under the cushion; I had a feeling that I knew, but did I <u>really</u> know? Was I right, and, more importantly, did I really <u>need</u> to know at this proximity if I was right? Right, deep breath, think this through. It was unlikely that the police had been in, in my absence, so who was it? What was going on, who was sitting in that Audi out there? Who had been in my house; how had they gotten in, how had they gotten out, without a trace, and what had they done to my TV chair? Somehow, from here on, it was going to be pointless watching TV anyway. Well, I couldn't just sit here doing nothing. I need a plan.

Keeping clear of the chair, getting up, I retreated to the safety (only joking) of my kitchen.

Perhaps it was red wine, but I decided that I had to find out about the chair and its secrets; I could hear Mother telling me not to be stupid (brave), but I couldn't leave it for someone else to find. At least then I could either deal with it, or tell someone else how to deal with it.

In the bathroom, which was next to the kitchen, was a hanging rail that I hadn't got round to taking upstairs. I unscrewed the bottom rail and wheeled it, wobbling slightly, into the living room and positioned it over the chair. A thin metal skewer from the kitchen drawer and a ball of green, hairy string completed my tool kit, and I, warily, knelt in front of the chair. As gently as I could, drops of sweat dripping, I pushed the skewer into the top surface of the cushion, and out and in again, leaving a two-inch length of skewer exposed in the middle. Wiping the drips from my forehead, trying to stop my heart from exiting my chest, I rubbed my hands down my trousers to get rid of the sweat and trembling, before attempting to tie the string to the middle of the skewer. Then I ran the string over the top rail, and retreated to the kitchen door, letting the string run out behind me. Taking up the slack, I began to pull the string to lift the cushion.

The clothes rail began to slowly move towards the kitchen, legs beginning to splay further apart, because the rail holding them in position had been removed. The cushion stayed exactly where it was.

Time to think again.

Leaving the string to sag and trail across the living room, I lifted the television off its base, and placed it at an angle over the feet and wheels on one side of the stand. With the coffee table upended across the other end of the base, collecting string on the way, I, again, retreated to the kitchen. Pulling carefully on the string, this time, the stand stayed in place, and the cushion started to rise. When it was six inches clear of the chair, I tied the string to the radiator valve that was just inside the kitchen, and waited for the cushion to stop swinging.

I suppose you could call it a 'whoopee cushion', but in reality, it was a 1kg slab of Semtex, a detonator pushed into the slab, wired to a pressure pad that was lying on the top. With shaking hands, I pulled the detonator out of the slab. It was a bit thicker than a king size fag, and about as long. The connecting wires tightened, as I withdrew it, and, with trembling hands, managed to keep it from tensioning the connection to the pressure pad (if I hadn't, I wouldn't be telling you this bloody story – would I? And I think I would have noticed).

I sat back on the floor, got my breathing back under control, and managed to stop my hands from playing the imaginary piano.

Dumping everything on the kitchen table, I sat and stared at the collection of bits, waiting for them to tell me who had put them together.

There was really only one answer.

Chapter 35

12th June 1998

I had never been able to get rid of the crampons, ice axe, and mouldy survival crap that I had carried around, unused, for years. I could never accept that I was never going up that mountain again, never going to kick into the ice, never going to hand-jamb into that crevice, or put the right nut in the crack that will hold when I fall (you need to have done it to understand). So, I had transferred it all from house to house, garage to garage, bin bag to bin bag. Having recently retrieved my sentimental 'treasures' from my ex 'man cave', I knew where everything was, and which bits to pack.

The Karrimor 65ltr rucksack was worn, used, abused, and could tell stories better than me. Ignoring the ice stuff (it was June after all), I stuffed bin liners, Crunchie bars, clothes, pants, socks, passport, Semtex, detonators, pressure switch, 9mm Browning, and ammunition into my sack; what a mixture.

I was startled back into reality by my phone ringing.

John, my Brother-in-law, launched into me without preamble: "What the hell is going on, Sam?"

"Oh! Hi John. Err, it's a bit complicated; you know about Jane, I guess, and that the police are convinced that I did it."

"And did you?" John interrupted.

"I could be offended, mate, but I suppose you had to ask."

"So, did you?"

"No, of course I didn't."

"So, where are you with the police then?"

"Well, I'm not charged with anything, but they have 'asked' me not to leave the area. I'm not really sure where that leaves me, other than still being a suspect."

"So, if not you, who did it then, and why?"

"I don't know, John, but ..." I let the sentence hang and trail off, whilst I thought about what to say.

Interrupting my thoughts, John said: "What aren't you telling me, then?"

"I'm not sure, John, but I think this is about something in my past that is nothing to do with Jane, nothing to do with reality; it has nothing to do with anyone in my family, and, at the moment, you are better off not knowing, and not being involved. Just distance yourself and the family as far away from me as you can, until I sort this shit out. Just keep everyone away from me, and keep Mother away from it all."

"Sounds like total bollocks to me, Sam." John was always diplomatic in his approach to 'issues'. "Just tell me what's going on, Sam, cut the bullshit!"

"It might seem like total bollocks to you, John, but I'm not going to put anyone else at risk; I can't take the chance. I accept that I might be wrong, but I'm going to get out of the way for a while, so that I can sort all this out without involving everyman and his dog."

"If you haven't done anything, why are you hiding, why take yourself away?"

"I know you will find this difficult to understand, but... just for once, accept that I know what I'm doing and trust me. Keep Mother away from it all, keep all the kids close, and look after everyone."

"Sam! You're a fucking fantasist; get back to reality, what are you doing about the funeral?"

"To be honest, I haven't thought about it. Anyway, the body hasn't been released yet, so there's nothing we can do. Please don't give me the hypocritical shit because nobody in the family liked Jane when she was alive, and she didn't exactly 'embrace' the family, did she?"

"What do you mean 'we'? She was your bloody wife; you sort the funeral stuff, it's not my problem!"

"Just back off, John, I don't need you on my case as well, just look after Mother, stay away from me, and I'll sort this mess out."

I disconnected the call before he could say anymore. I had to think quickly, make some decisions; there could be a knock on the door any minute, and I would have to explain 1kg of Semtex and a Browning (not to mention a browning in the trouser department).

I left the cottage through the back door, dumped the rucksack on the passenger seat, and drove out of the car park down the narrow alley to the main road, turned left and headed north. Glancing right as I merged with the traffic, I caught a glimpse of the black Audi. It was a few cars back from the junction this time, but I was fairly sure it was the same one. Turning right, right and right again, I joined the road where the Audi was parked and drove towards it. It appeared to be unoccupied, and I had time to see in my headlights the first digits of the registration S736. I drove passed it, stopped at the junction, and glanced in the mirror. My brake lights reflected on something pale and light in the screen of the

Audi – and it moved; there was someone in it, and they were clearly trying not to be seen. I turned right, and set off north again, watching the rear view carefully for the Audi. It was nearly 1 o'clock in the morning, and I needed to get going, but held my speed so that I could see if the car followed me.

After half a mile, I pulled into a lay-by and waited, lights off, engine running, two minutes, three minutes, no Audi. A small car passed, and then pulled into a drive way a few hundred yards further on. I was quite calm now, I was getting used to this. I had a plan – a sense of purpose, a destination, and it had quite a calming effect. I also now had a determination, and was not going to let these people beat me; I was going to win this game, if I could just put the pieces together.

My calmness was short lived as I pulled out of the lay-by, and, as the car lurched over a pothole, the seat belt alarm startled me momentarily. What the ... then I realised that my car thought that my passenger should fasten his seatbelt, and, with a momentary chuckle, I reached over, dropped the rucksack into the foot well, and drove on.

Now, confidant that I was on my own, I put my foot down; I had an hour or so to get to the truck stop on the M6, and find the man I was looking for.

I did a quick tour of the lorry park, spotted the trailer that I was looking for, and knew that he would be arriving in the next 20 minutes or so to collect it. I parked on the car park in a dark corner, and headed into the café via the gents. Then, into the café, ordered a coffee and a double cheeseburger, and settled to wait. The television in the corner was on the news channel, full of the latest from Afghanistan and the inevitable collateral damage that seems to upset everyone. Why don't people realise that you can't have a war that only kills the bad guys? I went back to my burger, and the cholesterol damage.

It was approaching 2 a.m., so I thought I should get myself organised and go back to the car to get my rucksack. Even at this time in the morning people were around – trucks were constantly pulling in and pulling out, and some weary car travellers too. The central locking clunked, lights flashed, and I reached in, retrieved my rucksack, and sat in the car, thinking about what else I should take, or secure, before abandoning it. Satisfied that I'd not forgotten anything, I locked up, slung the bag over my shoulder, and walked around the car and tried all the doors. I don't know why I did it, I knew it had central locking, but, because it was going to be here for a while, it just felt better to be sure.

As I tried the tailgate, I saw it. I tried not to show any sign of recognition, tried not to stop dead in my tracks, tried not to drop my jaw, tried not to show any shock, tried not to get back in the car, tried not to drive like a lunatic into the night. The Audi was parked three rows in, facing me. Calmly, (yeh right), I walked away thinking quickly, how the hell have they got here? I wasn't followed, I knew I hadn't been followed, nobody knew where I was, where I was going, I hadn't spoken to anyone, brother in-law John was the last person I'd spoken to, and I hadn't said anything to him. SHIT! mobile phone tracking; you idiot.

I went back to the gents into a cubicle, put the bag on the floor and listened. No footsteps; they seemed to be happy to just keep track of my car and mobile, not me. That's ok, I thought, I just need to separate me from my phone, but do I go back and just dump the phone in the car? I sat, thought, made a decision, and, because I was running out of time, took a risk.

I left the gents, and walked back onto the lorry park, scanned the assembled trucks and waited. A Romanian registered truck was parked close to where I was standing, the driver walking around it, checking his trailer, before setting off. It was a curtain sided trailer with a security cord locking all the strap buckles. As he walked around to the rear, I casually walked along the side, pulled the bottom edge of the curtain away from the edge of the trailer bed, and slipped my phone in, and onto, the trailer bed. We met at the front of his truck, and I said: "Hi mate, you going north or south?"

"I go Scotland", he said.

"OK, mate, that's no good for me." …and I walked back into the café.

Pete Lloyd was sitting at the back of the café with a coffee, watching the television. I dumped my bag on the floor, sat down and said, "Can I have a lift, mate?"

"Sorry, mate. Sam! What the hell are you doing here? Good to see you. How the hell are you?"

"I'm good, Pete, but I need a lift. I assume you're still doing the Cardiff trunk, and I could do with a lift down as far as the M50."

"You know I'm not allowed to carry passengers, but I guess you don't count, seeing as you were the boss when the rule was introduced," he said.

"You and I both know that you wouldn't hesitate if I was wearing a short skirt and needed a hand to get up into the cab, Pete!" I said, with a grin.

"Honestly, Sam, you would have no chance if you were wearing a skirt, no matter how short it was, but I get the point. So, where are you headed?"

Thinking quickly, I said: "I'm actually trying to get to Hereford to pick up a car I've bought."

"Are you going to try and thumb it from Strensham then?" He asked, and then, without waiting for a reply, said "Why don't you come down to the depot (Cardiff) and jump on the Mid Wales van"?

"I hadn't thought of that, Pete, but I don't want get involved with anyone from the Depot; there's a lady in the finance office that I used to 'know', and her husband used to work nights in the traffic office, and probably still does. Who's doing the Mid Wales run nowadays?"

"Don't worry, mate", with a wink, he said "It's a new-ish guy on that run, so he won't know any history. I'll tell him you're a mate. I'll drop you on the 470 and get Danny to pick you up at the petrol station".

Over the next three hours we talked about how the company had changed, about the 'tosser' (his term, although I agreed), who had taken over from me, and that my successor was known as The Rug Rat because of his connections with the carpet industry. We talked about Pete's latest relationship issues, and about Karen, the love of his life; although it was a bit of a one-sided conversation, it was good to hear that the 'empire' was progressing without me.

My mind wandered to the Audi, the Romanian trucker, the contents of my rucksack, my brother-in-law John, Mother, and back to the Audi … and at several points, I slept.

Chapter 36

12th June 1998

In Cheshire, the office door opened, and a head appeared. "He's running, boss, and the Spooks are in a panic. They want a meeting, now!"

Neil Maynard put his pen down, and said: "OK, Bob, where are they? Are they in the Ops room or Conference"?

"Conference, and they've got the Army lads with them too."

Standing, DI Maynard took a thick file from his desk drawer. "I'll be there in a sec, Bob, Oh! Take a coffee in for me, would you, mate? I'm getting too old for being up all night."

"Sure." The head disappeared.

In the Conference room were six men; Neil Maynard knew all of them. Two of them, Mike and Phil were Army, or ex-Army, George Bennett he knew was SAS and Mike and Phil's boss effectively, but the reporting lines were a bit blurred. Dave Rogers and the dour Scot, Philip Stewart-Rae were both SIS (MI6) Officers. He and his colleague, DS Bob Williams, represented the local Police Force.

Neil nodded a greeting, dropped his file on the long table, sat next to Bob Williams and said: "Thanks Bob" as he picked up the coffee. "So, where are we, gentlemen?" He asked the assembled stern faces. Of them all, only Mike smiled as a greeting, the rest were stony faced. PSR, as Stewart-Rea was known, didn't hesitate.

"This is a shambles, Maynard, your backwater bobbies couldn't organise a piss-up; you've lost him, and we are in deep shit."

Mike (OB), without a surname, who was one of the Army contingent, said "Hang on, a sec, we are not dealing with a muppet here, Philip; this guy knows what he's doing, and you shouldn't underestimate him. It's not surprising that he sold us a dummy and 'did one'. Let's not beat each other up over it. We just need to find him, and quickly."

"Is someone going to tell me what's going on?" Maynard asked, "I get that we've lost him, but how? What happened?"

"Neil, it's our fault" Phil explained, "We told your man to hang back, and not follow him because we were tracking his phone, but he sussed it somehow, and ditched his phone on the M6; we caught up with it just over the border in Scotland because Mike smelt a rat and knew it wasn't his patch."

"Enough of this." PSR said, slapping his hand on the table in frustration. "We need to find him before this turns to rat-shit; sorry to beat you up, Neil, but this is a major problem." There was a pause, whilst everyone gathered thoughts, and desperately tried to think of a recovery plan. Phil broke the silence.

"He's been up all night. We've been up all night. He'll be having a kip somewhere, and I would suggest we do the same and reconvene in the morning."

"It IS fucking morning" muttered Mike, to no one in particular.

"Yes, ok." PSR said: "Let's have a fresh look at it in the morning", glancing at Mike as if challenging him to contradict him. "Let's see what Intel comes in, and we'll meet again at, say, 10 hundred?" It was posed as a question, but didn't need an answer. He looked for agreement from the silent and thoughtful Dave Rogers, caught his eye, and acknowledged the nod of agreement from him.

Files and cups were gathered, backs were stretched, stubble was rubbed, and the room was vacated.

Two hundred miles away, and exactly one hour earlier, Vasile Gafengu was beginning to feel the strain of driving from Dover to Glasgow in one hit. His fictitious co-driver had been no help, other that the use of his name on the card in the Tachograph that recorded the driving hours. If he could get to Chaplehall by eight o'clock, he was in with a chance of collecting his return load from Sunderland the same day, and then he could relax and get some sleep.

"Pula Mea!" He shouted, as he saw the flashing yellow lights ahead, then brake lights as the traffic was funnelled into the nearside lane. Fortunately, the traffic wasn't too heavy at that time in the early the morning, and he was relieved to see that traffic was rejoining the motorway, after temporarily stopping at whatever this hold up was. The flashing lights were giving him a headache, and all he could see were Hi-Vis jacketed 'officials' who were waving traffic around some sort of hazard that must have obstructed the motorway.

The truck in front moved off, and he drove slowly forward to the instructions of a Hi-Vis jacket. He stopped, as indicated, with a hiss of air brakes, and everyone moved to the other side of the traffic queue, because his truck was left-hand drive. He dropped his window and smiled, trying to look confident and at ease, hoping that this would not involve checking his driving hours.

"Do you speak English?" He was asked.

"Little", Vasile replied. Yet another Hi-Vis appeared, this one holding a laptop, and he nodded at the other Hi-Vis.

"Can you get out, please?" This was accompanied by gesticulations, just in case "get out" was not understood. Vasile opened the door, and, turning to face the cab, began the climb out down the three steps.

To say his feet didn't touch the floor isn't quite true. They did, but not before his arse, back and head, as he was descended upon by four black clad figures.

Vasile was late for his unloading at Chaplehall.

Chapter 37

9th June 1998

Three days before, Sam's wife, Mrs Jane Burgess, had a million thoughts flashing through her mind in milliseconds.

Did she hate him? Yes and no.

Did she care what happened to him? No and yes.

Did she want to kill him? Yes, most of the time.

Did she want someone else to kill him? No! Of course not, but....Yes! Possibly, maybe. No! Well, err...

Did she want to hurt him, inflict pain and devastate his life like he had devastated hers? Bloody right she did. But the closest she'd got was merely to cut his passport into pieces: "See if that causes you a problem, you bastard! Deal with it."

It was such a shock to find out things about him that she had never dreamed of. She still couldn't get past the betrayal, the deceit, the lies, and the horrendous shock that the devastating truth had battered and bludgeoned her almost into mental oblivion.

She remembered his words, though, at a subsequent meeting, when they were trying so hard to be 'civilised', when he said: "You should not have used 'withholding sex' as a weapon." It was painful, but she knew it was true.

Then, the arrival of a Police Inspector and a Security Services Officer had shocked her too. Yet more things she didn't know about him, 'matters of national security' seemed like total rubbish to her. Things like this don't happen in real life. She couldn't believe what they were telling her; it was just fantasy. Then, when she was handed the phone to talk to a Home Office Minister that she sort of recognised, but now couldn't remember the name of, she began to accept that this was real. The prat who introduced himself as SIS Officer Philip Stewart-Rae was just not credible, dark blue pin-stripe suit, red bow tie, brown suede shoes, really! With a blue suit? 'We don't all play Polo in Cheshire, you dick,' she thought. He was a caricature, something from a 'B' movie, too far up his own arse to be taken seriously.

DI Maynard was something else, though; quietly spoken, confident, believable, and 'dishy'. He instilled confidence, what he was saying was given more credibility because he had a voice like melting dark chocolate. When he said that she had no choice, and that she had to do what they were asking, she believed him. 'I'll do whatever you want me to do', she thought. She accepted his reassurances that they (her and the dogs), would be temporally relocated in a safe place, in a country house. No expense spared, dogs running free in the forest, free to chase rabbits, squirrels or anything else, whilst she would have access to a luxury Spa, the best food, wine and Five Star accommodation, in exchange for being totally out of contact for 'a few days'.

'Will you be included, DI Maynard?' she thought. 'No, don't fantasise about room service, Jane'.

She expected them to come back the next day to collect her and the dogs, and was totally thrown when the policeman said that she was to pack clothes, medication, the dogs' toys, whatever else she deemed essential, and would be vacating her home in the next 10 minutes.

"Can I ring around and just say I'm going away for a few days? What about my son, what about my family? I can't just disappear like this; they will be frantic if I disappear without telling them I'm going away – they will ring the police and... Oh! Yes, I see. So, what will you tell them, Inspector?"

"Don't worry about that, Mrs Burgess, we will ensure that they are not alarmed by your temporary absence, and we will allow communication between you and your family as soon as we are able. Now, I need to ask you to gather your things together very quickly. I have a female Liaison Officer outside who will help you."

"I don't need any help, thanks."

"Well, to be honest Jane, she has another role, which is to ensure that you do not inadvertently pack something that can be traced and divulge your location to the people that we are trying to protect you from, so I'd appreciate it if you would allow her to assist you with your packing. We are really grateful to you for your help and co-operation, but this is really important for your safety, and the safety of our local community."

It was rumoured that, sometime later, Margaret Thatcher stayed in this hotel whilst she wrote her memoirs; probably because of its isolated, and therefore secure, location.

The three cars crunched slowly to a halt on the gravel, as two porters descended the steps to open car doors, remove bags and assist their valued guests to make themselves comfortable enough not to worry about the amount of money they were about to spend. Speech and greetings were halted, as a helicopter rose from the pad behind the hotel, having delivered, or collected, other guests. The dogs were spooked by it, prancing about, and entangling Jane in dog leads, which almost led to an ungainly, and decidedly unglamorous, entrance (as in arse over t'dog). Neil Maynard held her elbow and helped untangle her, insisting that the porters took charge of the dogs (who had now realised that pursuit of the helicopter was pointless).

In the palatial entrance, and main hotel reception area, she was told that registration was not required, that all expenses were to be charged to her room. She was handed her key card, and directed to the lift. Turning toward the lift, she was 'confronted' by DS Sue Vaughan, her Liaison Officer.

"Sorry, Jane, can I have your phone, please?"

Jane shot an enquiring look towards DI Maynard, who smiled and nodded reassuringly. She reluctantly handed over her only contact with the rest of the world.

Chapter 38

11th June 1998

As darkness descended on Mrs Jane Burgess's now empty house, the tired and weary figure with the bag over his shoulder, trudged past. Glancing briefly at the black Range Rover parked under the trees, seemingly without recognising the significance; he walked on. Head down, he now passed the second Range Rover that was parked a little further on up the road in the entrance, next to the Undertaker's. Turning left, the figure faded from the view of the black clad driver in his rear view mirror. He walked on, turning through the houses, turned again onto the main road, and back to the centre of the village, where he had parked.

Passing his car, pausing only to drop his bag onto the back seat, 'clunk', flash of indicators, car locked, he walked into the village pub, the centre of all knowledge and gossip. He ordered a pint, and stood at the bar with the 'locals', who were arguing about the merits of the soon-to-be imposed, new one-way system in the village. He knew not to initiate any conversation, just make eye contact, smile, and await the invitation from them. It came quite quickly when, beginning to lose the argument, the guy in the paint spattered overalls turned to him.

"What do you think, mate, do you think it will make it worse?"

"Sorry, I don't know enough about the village to say. I'm just here to see if I can find a mate who I think used to live around here."

"Who's that then?"

"Sam Burgess, do you know him?"

"Yeah, we know him, but he's moved now – had a woman problem, and he split with his misses. He used to live just up the road and came in here a lot." Turning away, "Andy! You got Sam's new address? You're supposed to be decorating his new place, aren't you?"

"Don't know the address, but it's number eight in that row of cottages on the left as you get to the top of the hill, just as you get into Bartrum village. I've got his phone number in the van if you want it?"

"No that's ok, I know where you mean, I'll track him down one day. So, are they putting traffic lights in at the junction, or altering the round about?"

Nick didn't listen to the answer, just nodded and looked interested, as the debate at the bar moved on and became more animated. He finished his pint, waited for a suitable crescendo in the argument, and mumbled: "Thanks and goodnight, Gents", and left un-noticed, and instantly forgotten, by the 'one-way system' debaters.

Back at his car, he got in, and reached for the map in the back pocket of the passenger seat. He wrote a note at the side of the map, 'N8 – cottages left   top of hill', and set off to the village.

He spotted the cottages straight away, saw the street name on the road sign, circled round, and drove past again before parking outside a newsagent across from a take-away. He crossed the road and went in. The Chinese lady greeted him with a toothless smile, which made her look as if she was in pain.

"Watt u want?" Was the greeting.

"Do you deliver in the village?"

"Yes, one pound charge, if less five pounds."

"Great, can I have a menu, please?"

Menu in hand, he went back to his car, got in, and drove back to the road opposite the cottage. He parked in a row of cars, so that he had a clear view of number eight, and switched off the engine and the lights, and waited. Number eight was in darkness; no one was around. All was quiet. He picked up the menu and his phone, selected chicken curry with fried rice and prawn crackers, rang through the order, asked the price, requested delivery to the back door of number eight, and waited.

After five minutes, he collected his bag from the back seat, got out, locked the car and walked away from the car and the cottage, round the block, approaching the cottages from the other direction. Walking purposefully down the alley at the side of number nine, he turned behind the rear of the cottages, and melted into the shadows.

The sound of the moped coming down the alley was louder than it should have been; clearly the rider had no consideration or understanding of 'peace and quiet', only concerned with achieving his 'mission' as quickly as possible. He turned in a circle, stopping at the rear gate, foot stand down, he got off, leaning the moped onto the stand. Opening the lid of the box on the back, he took out the insulated bag, walked up the path to the backdoor, and knocked.

He waited, knocked again, this time more vigorously, and waited some more. With muttering and more knocking, he waited. Then, kicking the door in frustration, he turned to face Nick.

"Sorry, mate, you got here before me." He gave the lad ten quid, and said: "Keep it, buddy, sorry I kept you waiting", and, taking the white carrier bag from him, stepped to one side, as the now late delivery driver (rider) took the money.

"Thanks, enjoy".

"I'll shut the gate, ta!" Nick said, and, having done so, put the bag on the path, opened the side pocket on his bag, and removed the lock picks. It was a simple, three lever mortice lock that took him ten seconds – and he was in. He was out again in less than ten minutes, having spent most of the time looking at options. Once he had confirmed that the cottage was empty, he found the light switch in the living room, deciding that the main light would attract less attention that a flashing torch. He could see the normality of Sam's existence, looked at the chair in front of the computer: dismissed it. He looked at the toilet in the bathroom: dismissed it. He considered a trip wire across the kitchen door: dismissed it. Front door: dismissed it, and then saw the sagging upholstery of the chair in front of the TV. With a smile, he pictured the result of leaving his package there, and opened his bag. He was practiced and confident; it took no more than two minutes to place it, he was, however, very careful when replacing the cushion.

Locking the door behind him, he retrieved the carrier bag, closed the gate quietly, and climbed over the fence at the back of the car park. He walked along the edge of the field eating the, surprisingly, still warm curry with his fingers. At the end of the field, he discarded the remains of the take-away, wiped his fingers on the considerately provided napkin, and climbed over the gate and on into the lane.

It took another fifteen minutes for him to get back to his car via this meandering route, all the time wondering if he would hear the explosion before he got there. He wanted the refuge that his car represented before that happened, but was disciplined enough to know that the direct route was not the safest option, and neither was walking fast or running. He walked casually, and when he met a couple walking towards him, he stopped, turned away from them, and whistled his imaginary dog, before walking on.

Now back in the warmth of his car, he waited.

It was over an hour before the approaching headlights swung into the alley-way instead of continuing past as all the other dozen cars had done. There was a passing of several minutes whilst his heart rate increased. He swallowed, sweating now, not from fear, but excitement. This was actually new for him; he had always just put them in place and 'got the hell out', but this was different and important. He would have preferred to be close and personal, prefer to actually watch the light go out when he died, to see the fear, to feel his terror in the moment, the punishment, the final retribution. It would have been difficult to explain what it was like to actually kill someone in a way that allowed you to look into their eyes as life left them, as the light went out, as they faded away into oblivion. He waited.

The light increased at the window, and he pictured the kitchen light being switched on. After what seemed like an hour, but was only five minutes, the light came on in the living room. Then the bedroom light came on, and then off. Another few minutes, and the light went off in the living room and the curtains opened slightly at one side, back-lit from the light in the kitchen, a pause, curtains replaced, and the light came back on in the living room. He had a picture of Sam going from room to room, investigating; checking and looking through the windows, had he found it? He waited for the windows to explode, for the flash of light, the smoke, the smell of burning, and ... nothing.

Five more minutes passed, then ten, still nothing. He was still sweating, still expectant, but was beginning to calm as the realisation came to him that he had failed; Sam had somehow escaped his trap.

He thought through the options. What would he do now: 'Put yourself in his place' Nick thought. 'If it was me, I'd run and hide, go somewhere safe', so wait. Another half hour passed, lights appeared again upstairs, and then went out again. Finally, the light went out in the living room, and then the fainter light in the kitchen went out. 'Here we go,' Nick thought, and, after a few more minutes, Sam's Passat Estate's headlights appeared in the alley, stopped at the road and turned left, out of the village, and towards the motorway.

He needed to give Sam some space. Sam would be watching his mirror. He would be expecting to be followed. He started the car, and waited, thinking through his options. As he was about to pull out, a car approached from behind him, slowly, and he waited.

He recognised it as Sam's car, and couldn't believe how close he had come to buggering up his surveillance. As it passed, and turned right at the junction, he was momentarily distracted when a car, an Audi, previously parked three cars ahead, started; it switched its lights on, pulled out and away – a flash of brake lights as it stopped at the junction, and then turned left, in the opposite direction to that which Sam's Passat had gone, and disappeared.

He thought for a moment about that car, and decided that he had been too focused on the cottage to see anyone getting in it before driving off. Leaving the village, he headed in the direction Sam had taken. There were a few bends and side roads to negotiate, but then the road was straight, and he could see probably half a mile ahead, – the road was clear. Thinking logically, Nick reckoned that a Passat would not have been able to get that far ahead of him in the lapsed time to be out of sight, and thought that he must have turned off somewhere in the village. Not being too familiar with the village, he slowed and thought about his next move 'How do I get back on his track?' He was approaching a lay-by, and, as he passed it, he could see that a car was parked, lights off, but with exhaust fumes rising, engine still running. 'Got yer!', he thought, and drove past and waited in the driveway of a house set back from the road.

After a few minutes, the Passat pulled out, going towards the motorway, he guessed. The road was straight for about a mile, and, taking a chance, he switched his lights off, pulled out and followed. He hung back, learning from his training in Ireland and

Libya, waited until the traffic lights changed, and for the Passat to move off, signalling a right turn. He switched his lights on, floored his 'tuned' Golf GTI, and got to the lights as they changed to red, using all of the 190 bhp. Ignoring the lights, he also turned right, tyres squealing in protest, heading for the motorway, and then immediately slowed so that he didn't catch up to the Passat.

Nick drove slowly, then accelerated to catch up, then drove slowly again, always keeping some distance, but not losing sight, until the Passat turned into the truck stop car park. He had still to see Sam's face, still to recognise him for the future, and was comfortable with Sam not recognising him and compromising his own anonymity.

Nick lost him, momentarily, and then saw his car; he appeared to be looking for a vehicle on the lorry park, but then returned to the car park, stopping in a dark corner. He'd parked close to the exit, some distance from Sam's car, but close enough to see what Sam was doing. He watched Sam get out, saw the lights flash as he locked it, and watched him walk towards the café. Nick followed, and, from a distance, watched as he ordered food, and then sat and started to eat.

Nick didn't go in; he loitered, pretending to talk on his phone, whilst watching Sam through the window. Sam looked at his watch, stood, and Nick, sensing that he might be leaving, decided to go back to his car in case Sam had decided to drive out. He got back to his car in time to watch Sam open the door and get in, waiting for the engine to start, lights to be switched on – he got ready to follow. The car didn't start; Sam got out again, locked up, walked all round the car, and ambled off back to the café area, with a rucksack slung over his shoulder. There was a sort of finality about it, as if he wasn't coming back to the car. Nick pondered on this for a while, and then set off in pursuit.

He lost him again – wasn't in the café, couldn't see where he'd gone. He went back to the car park, no, he wasn't in his car, went back to the café and did another circuit, then to the lorry park, again, no sign of him. Checked the café again, checked the car park again, now, heart rate rising, he was beginning to realise Sam must have met up with someone and gone off in another vehicle, or maybe just walked out. Time for some food and a coffee, whilst he thought through the options. Standing at the counter waiting to be served, he spotted Sam coming in through the side door. He watched Sam stop and look around, and, when he'd spotted who he was looking for, he walked to the back of the café, dropped his bag on the floor, and immediately started talking to the man sitting there, who he clearly knew. They seemed like friends, but he got the impression that it was an unexpected meeting.

Nick just got coffee and a pack of four pork pies, and sat as close as he dared, turned his back to them so that he faced the TV and sipped his coffee. He strained to try and hear as much as he could of the conversation. Sam spoke quietly, but he picked up bits from his friend: "Honestly, Sam, you would have no chance..." then, "...thumb it from Strensham then?", pause, "Why don't you come down..." The rest was lost as music started on the TV. Nick had heard enough; this was a trucker that Sam knew. He was hitching a ride to somewhere, and all Nick needed to do was identify the truck that Sam was getting into, and he was sorted.

Leaving the remains of his coffee, he walked out onto the lorry park, found a spot away from the security light, and stood in the shadows to wait. After ten minutes, Nick was beginning to feel a bit exposed; he didn't want to attract attention to himself, lurking suspiciously around the parked trucks. He was relieved when the two appeared, chatting amiably, as they walked to the bright yellow Scania tractor unit, hitched to the equally bright yellow trailer, parked next to another yellow trailer, which was without a unit attached to it. 'Bingo', Nick said to himself; it won't be difficult to spot that on a crowded motorway.

Chapter 39

12th June 1998

The petrol station on the outskirts of Cardiff had a café area attached, but was only DIY drinks machines and a microwave. It only had three customers, including me; all of us were immersed in our own thoughts. I looked around, and felt reasonably secure and anonymous. I took my paper cup of coffee to a corner table from where I could see the fuel pumps, the entrance beyond, about 300 yards of the main road, and the café customers.

I guessed that I had about half an hour before the van driver arrived, as long as Pete had persuaded him to pick me up. I thought through the 'what if' scenarios – what I would do if he didn't appear. My plan was to give him an hour, and then would try and get a lift back into town and hire a car, but that was going to be a last resort, because I wanted to conserve my limited remaining cash, and thought that I would have to pay on a card anyway. A car hire company wouldn't want to give a car to someone paying cash who didn't want to give a name and address. I knew that, inevitably, I was going to leave a trail that the police could follow, but they were not my biggest concern. At least Billy One wouldn't know where I was. He had managed, somehow, to find me in Cheshire, and I wondered how. I thought that he would also eventually track me down, but at least this time I'd be ready for him.

My thoughts were interrupted by the approaching headlights of the van as it turned off the road, and slowly drove though the pumps, and stopped just before the exit. I recognised the livery, and knew straight away that it was Pete's mate. Leaving my now cold coffee, I scooped up my bag and left. He was getting out, and, as I approached, held out a hand.

"You must be Sam?"

"Hi Danny, Pete said you would give me a lift to Hereford; hope that's ok?"

"Sure, no problem – jump in. I'm a bit late, so need to get going." Nothing was said for the first few miles. Then: "Whereabouts do you want to be in Hereford, Sam?"

"Anywhere in the middle of town, but I really want to be as close as you can get me to the railway station – there is a garage near there where I have to pick up a car, so close as you get me, really."

"I know it's a bit off route, but I can drop you at the junction just before it. It's only half a mile or so, but that's the best I can do, coz I'm a bit behind this morning, still learning the job really. That ok?"

"Brilliant, Danny. That's great, thanks." The rest of the one hour trip passed with small talk about Danny's life history – none of which I took in.

My memory of Hereford was a bit out of date, but I remembered a second-hand car dealer who 'specialised' in cheap cars, and I suspected that cash would be very acceptable. Risky as it was, I knew that the first stop would have to be the cash point, and I drew £200 on my debit card and another £300 on my credit card. With the cash I already had, that gave me £900 with which to get wheels, and enable me to exist for the next few days, or would it be weeks. I would have to be 'careful' with money, I thought, as I walked away from the cash point. This extravagant expenditure is going to be difficult to explain to Jane. I stopped mid-stride as the realisation hit me; Jane was dead, and I really had loved her. For a moment, I leaned against a shop window, and tried to swallow the emotion along with the lump in my throat. I blew my nose, gave myself a bollocking, shook myself, and walked on.

The car dealer's site was deserted, but I stepped over the chain that surrounded the parked cars, and wandered about looking at the various options. 'Think practical and inconspicuous', I told myself. 'Think reliable, think suitable for purpose. Think cheap.' Nothing inspired me, but, reaching the rear of the parked vehicles, I saw a 3 Series BMW with fading paintwork and tarnished chrome. The sign said '*1992, 160K ex-company car, Full service history £899*'. That was what I needed, something that had been serviced to death, and would have been looked after by a dealership. The 160 thousand miles was high, but would be ok for my needs. My watch said that it was eight thirty; my stomach said it was lunchtime, so I stepped back over the chain and went in search of bacon.

Across from the railway station was a café with a newsagent's next door, so I bought a paper and went for breakfast. I scanned through the paper, looking for news of the murder in Cheshire, and the manhunt for the suspected purp who was 'at large' – and found nothing. I wondered about that for a while, and then lost myself in eggs, bacon and 'local' Welsh sausage, and, for ten minutes, was oblivious to everything but my hunger and my breakfast. I'd forgotten how long it had been since my burger of the previous night/morning, and was suddenly overcome by the tiredness – I felt very heavy-eyed and tired.

I had another black coffee with lots of sugar, and tried to focus and stay awake. After an hour, I left the café, and, unfastening my fleece, let the cold morning air chill me into wakefulness. Stopping off at a phone shop, I asked for the smallest 'pay as you go' phone that they had on offer, bought it and put £20 worth of credit on it, stuffed it (minus packaging) into my pocket, and walked on. By the time I got back to Norman's Car Sales it was approaching 10:15am, and, although the chains were still in place, I could see that there was movement inside the office.

Again, stepping over the chain, I meandered around the cars and eventually was accosted by a spotty-faced youth in a polished suit and stained tie, who said: "That's a real bargain, that one", nodding towards the Mercedes that I had inadvertently leaned against (priced at £2499).

"Out of my range, I'm afraid, but I'd be interested in the BM at the back. Is it MOT'd, and does it have any tax on it?"

"Er, not sure, I'll have to check, it only came in two days ago and it's not even been cleaned yet, but, if yer interested, I'll have a look at the records. Come into the office, and I'll pull the details on it for you. Would you like a coffee?"

I gave them my insurance details; yes, it had four months tax, and twelve months MOT, was guaranteed for six months, and was ready to drive away. We agreed a cash price of £700, and, at 12:30pm, I drove away, declining the offer of a post-sale car wash and valet. The straight six BMW purred along, and I was really happy with my purchase.

Leaving Hereford, I tried to remember the route to Mike's place, and was following signs for Knighton. Just for reassurance, I decided to stop and buy a map. I needed fuel anyway, and pulled into a sleepy rural garage in Wigmore. I filled the car to the brim, bought a local OS map, a Cornish pasty (in Wales?), a bottle of water, and, to, conserve my remaining cash, paid with my credit card, thinking that my current account would not take another £44 hit. Driving on, I stopped in the next quiet lay-by. I had a play with my new mobile phone, learned how to power it up, and how to make and answer calls. I plugged the charging lead into the cigarette lighter socket, put it on charge, and stuck it on the dashboard. I covered the map in pasty crumbs and water dribbles, sorted out where I was, the place I was going to, my route, and fell asleep.

Chapter 40

12th June 1998

I slept until late afternoon, oblivious to the passing traffic, and, after watering the bushes, drove on to Bleddfa, turning off the main road just before the bridge. I drove the car up the lane and stopped at the gate before the cattle grid, got out and opened it.

The bolt squealed as I pulled it back, and the gate grounded at the half-way point – all signs that it hadn't been opened for a while, which was reassuring. Driving through, I went 100 yards past the cottage to the junction of two tracks. The one to the left meandered through the moor-land and on up onto the mountain, and the other, the forestry track, was a more direct route up the mountain, through the pine forest, to the rim of the slate quarry. I turned the car round, and parked in front of the cottage, under the trees. I slung my rucksack over my shoulder, walked back, closed the gate, and leaned against it; I listened to the tinkling stream, smelled the pines, and felt safe for the first time in a few days. The light was fading now, still only early evening, but in the shadow of the forest and mountain beyond, it was gloomy; no street lights to come on around here.

The key was where it always was – fourth stone to the right of the door. As the lock clicked, I pushed the big, heavy door open, and was greeted with the smell of the wood burner, and a damp, musty smell of age – a bit of dampness and neglect as in 'unused', rather than 'not looked after'.

I fumbled around the wall to the right of the door, and found the light switch, and was astounded at the transformation of the place. It had certainly changed since my last visit – really thick rug on the floor in front of the fire, comfy leather settee facing it, book shelves on the back wall, TV, CD player, small table in the corner, door at the end of the room, but still the same rickety stairs to the mezzanine loft bedroom, best described as 'rustic'.

Closing the door behind me, dropping my bag on the settee, I explored more, opening the new (as in not seen it before), rear door of the living room, and my jaw dropped as I entered a pristine kitchen that hadn't existed on my last visit. In contrast to the image from the front, it was modern – all the stuff you would expect, including a double fronted Aga stove with a comfy looking chair in the corner next to it, a fridge/ freezer, washing machine, microwave, small table and two chairs in the corner, with a fishing rod propped up behind the table next to a new window that looked out over the moor.

There was now a bathroom off to one side of the kitchen, and a new back door. The key was in the lock, and, unlocking the door, I explored the back of the cottage, which was all new to me. None of this existed when I last visited, and I was amazed by the work that OB had done. It opened onto a small, decked area, with folded chairs and folded table propped against the rear wall, and, in the corner, a barbeque with a cover over it.

There was a panoramic view across the moor-land on which the sheep were nibbling at the sparse grass. It was idyllic, with the low sun still shining on the back of the cottage. Wandering back into the living room, I looked through the CDs, and found a David Ward MacLean CD; I spent a minute working out how to switch on the CD player, and then lost myself in 'Marianas'.

I sat on the settee for a while, just listening and relaxing, enjoying the peace of the place. Going back into the kitchen, I grabbed a dusty bottle of Shiraz from the wine rack, a glass from the cupboard, and went outside. I leaned on the rail next to the barbeque, unfolded the table and a chair, hooked the chair with a foot, dragged it to the table, and sat.

Blowing the dust from the bottle, I poured, watched the sheep, and listened to the music, breathing in the pine, clear air, and listened to the CD, accompanied and complimented by the sound of the water from the stream. Looking back into the kitchen, a shaft of late evening sunlight shone through the window, illuminating the cooker and the dancing dust that I had disturbed. A spider abseiled from the North Face of the Aga. I drained the bottle.

With a sigh, I stood, and set about securing the place from any (un)expected intruder.

Starting at the back, using some of OB's fishing line, I fixed a trip wire across the decking, and connected it to the inverted pressure pad (the one that I had recovered from my 'whoopee cushion'), in front of the back door. It was rigged so that any increase in the pressure resulting from treading on the wire would complete the circuit, and trigger the quarter kilo of Semtex that was wrapped around the bottle, now full of gravel. This Shiraz was now considerably more than 13.5%; it would have much more of a kick.

Then, opening the front door, I thought about the options, and decided that I should just set a warning trigger at the front to alert me of someone approaching, rather than scattering the innocent postman's remains over Llandrindod. It suddenly occurred to me that the next person to approach the cottage might just be Mike O'Brian; it was, after all, his place. Thinking that I should tell him that I'm here, and not to come in through the back door, I wracked my brain, trying to remember his number – but couldn't.

Then, a moment of inspiration, and I started looking through the papers in the kitchen drawers, nothing, and then, on the book shelves, amongst other papers, I found a delivery note for a fridge/freezer. It showed the cottage address, and a contact phone number to advise delivery time; it was a mobile number.

Sitting on the settee, I retrieved my new phone and dialled the number. I had to walk outside through the back door to get a signal. I waited; it connected, and rang only twice before being answered by the familiar voice.

"O'Brian?", with a slight uplift at the end of the name, so that it sounded like a question.

"It's Sam: Mike, how yer doin'?"

"Err! I'm ok, Sam, ta! How you doin'? You ok?"

"To be honest, mate, I've been better, got a bit of a problem. Do you remember giving me a present, in a tin, and warning me that I might need it one day?"

"Certainly do, Sam."

"Well, it's happened, and he's coming for me. Are you around or are you away somewhere?"

"No, I'm not away mate, but I'm a bit tied up, though, and need to get off the phone. I'm also a long way from you, so I'll see if anyone is around who can help with power tools. I've got your number in my phone, so I'll be in touch."

Still leaning against the rail by the barbeque, the call clicked off before I could say anymore. It was a surprisingly abrupt end to the call, and made me wonder if he was on a job somewhere uncomfortable, and hoped that my call had not been a problem.

Staring at the now blank screen didn't help, so I went back into the cottage and retrieved more fishing line, a selection of cup hooks, cable ties and clothes pegs, not really sure what I was going to do with them. I threw the phone onto the settee next to my rucksack as I passed, and opened the front door – thoughts now back to creating an alarm system.

My planning and scheming was halted when, after crossing the threshold bridge, immediately in front of the door, I was confronted by a hiker standing in the lane: rucksack, anorak, waterproof trousers with pockets everywhere, walking boots, map in hand, looking left, then right, then back to map, seemingly undecided which track to take, moor land or forest track. He seemed to sense my presence and turned, smiled and said: "Oh, Hi, I think I'm lost. Does this track to the right go to the village or is it the one to the left?"

"Are you trying to get to Bleddfa?"

"Yes, sorry to bother you. I've followed the footpath off the mountain, but can't work out where I am now, not sure which way the village is."

"Well, if you go through the gate, onto the road and turn left, the village is about half a mile, but be careful, there's no footpath."

"Thanks." Pause, "You must be Sam Burgess?"

"What... I... Erm...! Yes.... Erm...!" Map was now discarded to reveal a snub-nosed pistol.

"Hi Sam, I'm Billy Conlan, nice to meet you after all these years. Shall we go inside?"

Chapter 41

12th June 1998

I turned, walked into the cottage, mind in turmoil, what to do. I knew, once inside, he would have the upper hand. I had only seconds to decide what to do; he was still to cross the threshold bridge, we were only a few feet apart, it was my only chance – fight or flight, he had the gun, the control.

Decision!

Now!

He was going to kill me anyway.

I slammed the door as hard as I could, grabbed my bag from the settee, dashed through the kitchen, leaped over the rail at the end of the decking, and ran. My shoulders were tensed, waiting for the bullet in the back. Ahead was open moor land, no cover, to the left was open and exposed for a hundred yards until the road, and then no hiding place.

I went right, twenty yards to the tree line and the protection of the forest and the darkness it provided – my only option. I couldn't hear anything that told me where he was, he wouldn't get through the door easily. I guessed he would work his way around the cottage, the easy way would be for him to go left. I was going right. I was far enough away now to be able to find a place to cross the stream; I didn't hesitate. I couldn't jump it, too wide, so slid down the bank into the freezing water, fast flowing, and two feet deep. I had managed to get arms through the straps of the rucksack as I ran.

I scrambled up the opposite bank, pulling myself up on the tree roots and out. I followed the edge for a while, and then, with a quick glance down the track, no sign of Billy, ran across the open track, and into the trees on the other side. Now, in-between the moor track and the forest track, I ran on further into the trees. I plunged on, deeper and deeper into the forest, the pine needle carpet quiet under foot, just the occasional branch to step over to make as little noise as possible. The loudest noise was my breathing and my pounding heart, but I swerved left and right between the trees and bracken. It was getting steeper now, harder to keep running, and I was slowing, all the time wondering if he was behind me, was he gaining, was he following?

I wanted to run, but forced myself to stop, tried to control my breathing, and listened. There was no sound that gave his position away to me, or mine to him, gentle swishing of the trees, and the distant burbling of the stream below and to my left. I shrugged off the rucksack, got the Browning from the pocket, thumbed off the safety, and began to feel a little better, a bit more in control.

I had run with no plan, no destination, no objective other than my escape and survival. He was younger than me, probably fitter too. I had lost my fitness over the years, but still had the stamina that my time with Phil, all those years ago, had built up, and I still had my determination to stay alive. I put the rucksack back on, and moved on further up the mountain, slower now, moving cautiously, avoiding low branches and fallen trees. I thought through the options; stay in the forest, circle back to the cottage that I had considered safe (and now wasn't). Should I fight my way down to the village, or continue up the mountain to the quarry? I had a slight advantage in that I knew the tracks and paths, I knew what was ahead. I could stay out of sight at least until daylight came. I reasoned that my safest place to hide and rest was behind the stone wall that ran along the rim of the slate quarry. Beyond the wall was a small area of grass before the hundred foot drop into the black water at the base of the quarry. Going over the wall was not for the faint hearted, and I reasoned that he would hesitate to follow.

I had the Browning, I could use it, and, although out of practice, used to be a good shot. I mentally pictured Billy One in the sights of the Browning. The quarry wall was my refuge, where I would wait, take aim and end it. However, I've never killed anyone before.

And then there was Mike; he had said that he would get some of the Hereford lads across to help. It suddenly occurred to me, thinking back to the conversation we'd had on the phone, he hadn't asked where I was. Did he know I was at the cottage? How could he know that I was at the cottage? I thought about ringing him, and then realised my phone was still on the settee, unless Billy now had it. Not much of this made sense.

Moving on, I stopped frequently to listen, straining to hear the slightest sound that might alert me to Billy's presence. Was he following? Was he behind a tree, waiting? Was he on the forest track still over to my right somewhere? Was he over to my left on the moor path at the tree line? It was very dark now; progress was slow because I was almost feeling my way from tree to tree. At least Billy wouldn't be able to see me; he would be reliant upon sounds too. I was getting tired. The trees were thinning. I was confronted by rocks now, to scramble over. I was getting close to the tree line and the quarry rim.

Then, the night sky, stars, more light, and, ahead, the dark outline of the stone wall across the ten feet of empty space between it and the protection of the trees behind me. I dropped to the ground, and edged forward on my belly, crawling towards the wall, reluctant to leave the protection of the trees. It was silent; nothing moved other than the gentle swish of the trees above me. I waited, laying in the shadows, looking left, then right, waiting for any sign of movement, any sound that would betray his presence. Ahead, I could see the yellow sign attached to the wall, and, although, I couldn't read it I knew it said: *'Danger. Quarry. Deep Water. Do Not Enter.'*

After a long wait, I began to feel the cold of my wet legs and feet after wading through the steam. It had been fine whilst I was hiking up the mountain, but was now uncomfortable. Time to move; cautiously standing, taking small steps to the wall, looking left and right, I crossed the exposed emptiness to the wall. It was chest high, with a black, empty void beyond, to ice cold water and certain death if, after dropping the other side of the wall, I lost my footing, and slid on the grass slope into oblivion. I flicked the safety catch to on, and put the Browning in the pocket of my fleece, put my rucksack on top of the wall, and searched for hand and foot holds to climb up and over the wall.

"You must think I'm a fuckin' idiot, Sam." I sank to my knees, defeated, unable to understand how he had out-witted me, out-thought me, out-manoeuvred me, and was back in control. Suddenly, I was exhausted, had no fight left, unable to resist. The Browning was removed from my pocket, all pretence of resistance gone, all determination and stamina expended. "Let's walk back down the track this time, eh! It's easier than scrambling through the trees." I had no energy left, I was not a macho super man who could deal with this stuff, overcome the enemy, fight to the death and beat him to a pulp with bloody fists. Billy pulled me to my feet, grabbed my rucksack from the wall, and pushed me, stumbling down the track, back towards the cottage.

It was considerably easier going down the track, even though a bit rutted in places; it was lit by the stars and a cloudy moon. My thoughts went back to my phone conversation with Mike; would his mates have got to the cottage, would they be waiting to save me? I plodded on, an occasional shove of encouragement, leaden legs, desperately wanting to just lie down and die. Why didn't he just kill me here, isolated, unobserved, no witnesses? Like everything else about this, it made no sense. The track merged with the moor-land track and the cottage beyond.

All was as we had left it; my car under the trees, and now, for the first time, I saw another car parked beyond the gate facing the road. I was beaten, resigned, defeated, and, to my shame, I gave in, was complicit, obedient and tears started. I was pathetic; I had given up.

Chapter 42

12th June 1998

The walk back had been mostly about staying on my feet, about survival, not about fighting back. Entering the cottage was a relief, I just wanted to sit down; I didn't care what happened to me – just wanted rest and a cup of tea.

Inside, he told me to empty my pockets, patted me down with one hand, the other holding my Browning, which he kept out of reach.

"Sit!"

The DWM CD was on repeat, and still going, now aptly playing 'Lonestar Regrets', and I sank into the leather settee as instructed, and waited for the bullet. A quick glance over his shoulder then eyes back on me, walking backwards into the kitchen, still eyes on me, he pulled a chair into the living room, shrugged off my rucksack and his, sat down in front of me – calm, in control, and exuding total confidence. I, on the other hand, was not calm, not in control, not exuding anything but fear; I could smell it, and was fairly sure that he could too.

'Will it hurt?', I thought, I've never been shot before, seen it – seen the results of it; it must hurt, just do it to my head, kill me quick, don't want to see it happening,

I'll turn my back, don't want to see it coming, do it now, shit; this is going to be painful.

"You don't look well, Sam."

"No, I don't feel well, to be honest. You are sitting in front of me, pointing a gun at my face. You killed my wife. You killed my fucking dogs. How do you expect me to feel?" There was a long pause; he said nothing, looked around the room as if looking for inspiration, a puzzled expression, furrowed brow. I thought about making a lunge for the gun; the odds were against it. I didn't.

"I didn't kill your wife or your dogs. Why do you think that I did that?" I was confused.

"Why deny it? What difference does it make now? Why tell me you didn't do it?"

"Because I didn't. If I had, I would tell you that I had, and I would enjoy telling you that I had. I did not kill your wife, Sam." I could tell that he was telling me the truth, – don't know why, it just seemed like it was the truth. We both sat in silence for a while, both thinking through the implications of it. If it was true, if he hadn't killed Jane, who had?

"Why did you leave a box of crockery in my wife's house?"

"Same answer, Sam, I didn't!"

Why would Maynard have told me that he had? Billy is lying. What the hell is going on here? I thought through everything. The first appearance of Maynard. The first disclosure that Jane and dogs had been killed. Being accused of doing it. Being accused of leaving the box of crockery, the steadying arm, as I stumbled when told. Finding the whoopee cushion.

"Did you plant a bomb in my living room chair, Billy?"

"Yes, I did do that. You found it, didn't you?"

"Yes, I found it."

"My plans have changed since then, Sam; I've got a better idea now, so I'm glad you found it."

He put the gun into his left hand, his right into the pocket of his rucksack, and smiled.

"Relax; we are going to be together for a while yet, so I've got something that will help to calm you down." His right hand withdrew a small, plastic container from the pocket, which he tossed across to me; it landed on the settee.

"Open it!"

I fumbled a bit, but managed to open it to reveal a syringe, a red cap on the needle.

"Now, you can do it yourself, or I can do it for you, but if I do it, I'll have to hurt you first. Your choice, Sam."

I looked at the gun, now back in his right hand, his unwavering gaze, looked back at the needle, looked back at the gun, looked back at his eyes. I pulled the red cap off the needle, pulled up my shirt, pinched a handful of flesh at my stomach, stuck the needle in, and pushed the plunger in the hope that it would take me into oblivion.

He seemed to relax a bit then, looked around the room, taking in the contents and layout of the place. With a new sense of resistance, and an unwillingness to give in, I took the opportunity to move slightly to one side, got my hand on the phone that I had left on the settee, and stuffed it down the back of my trousers and into my pants.

I don't know what I'd injected but I was 'comfortable'. Calm now. Aware of where I was, and what I was doing, but I felt strangely removed from reality. I was incapable of making my own decisions, felt unable to do anything other than what I was told to do. I fought it, shook my head, and tried to focus, tried to remember who I was, where I was. It began to get worse, I spoke, but the words were not what I thought I'd said, unintelligible drivel, even I couldn't understand what I had said.

I was totally disorientated, I heard a voice, but it was distant, drowned to an extent by a rushing sound in my ears. "What's your name?" "Sammm." "Where do you live?" "Bartrummm." "What's your bank card pin number?" "10 66 666 6666."

I stood, unsteadily, as instructed, shuffled to the door; my legs would not do what I told them to do. I was aware of the change from warm air to cold air.

I'm in a car now.

I don't know why.

I felt a seat belt across my chest.

Too tight.

I can't breathe, need air, panic breathing, why am I here, dizzy, bright lights, arms don't work, too heavy, too heavy to lift.

Then more bright lights, then no lights, leaning first one way, then the other, distant voices again. Echoes.

The lights were mesmerising; I was on a rocket ship, flying through space, narrowly avoiding stars, swerving this way and that as they shot by, leaving a trail of light behind them. The rushing noise changed to a roar, I tried to shout above the noise but what I heard was in my head, my mouth wouldn't open to release the words.

Chapter 43

13th June 1998

Neil Maynard started the update: "We've had hits on his bank cards; he drew cash from an ATM in Hereford, and he paid for a transaction at a petrol station in Mid Wales, some place called Wigmore, wherever that is. Mike is convinced that he knows where Sam is headed, Mike?" Mike looked around at the assembled, tired faces.

"I have a cottage out there that Sam has visited several times, but not for a while; it's remote, secluded, and he'll feel safe there. He knows the place, knows how to get in. He has permission to use it whenever, and it's ideal for him if he is trying to get off the radar. It's also ideal for us to bring Billy Conlan to it, too: no neighbours, no danger to civilians in the area; it couldn't be a better place for us to take Billy out, but I don't know how to get him there."

"Any ideas, Phil?" PSR asked.

"No, not right now. I can't leak it in the same way. It's just not credible; it would blow the whole thing. I don't see why Neil would be emailing me with a new location for Sam at this stage. Our friends would smell a rat, and probably warn Billy off; we'd lose him completely." As he started to speak, all eyes went to the SIS man Dave.

"He's in your patch, George; can you get a team down there now and take a look at Mike's place, but stay 'hands off' until we get a bit more info, and until we can think of a way of getting Billy there?"

"We have a team on stand-by, I'll make the call. Give me the location, Mike. We should be there within a couple of hours, and I'll get a sit-rep as soon as we are 'eyes on'." Mike scribbled, tore a page from his pad, and slid it across the polished table top. George stood, swept up the paper, and left the room.

Mike's phone rang. He glanced around the table, apologetically saying: "Sorry, I'll get rid of this." He pressed the button on his phone, said: "O'Brian." Paused, then standing, he held his hand, fingers spread, signalling to the assembled faces, saying "Err! I'm ok, Sam, ta! How you doin', you ok?"

There were meaningful looks exchanged. "Certainly do, Sam." Mike glanced at the faces, relieved that they could only hear his answers, not what Sam was saying. It would be difficult for him to explain the lethal shortbread tin. "No, I'm not away, mate, but I'm a bit tied up, though, and need to get off the phone. I'm also a long way from you, so I'll see if anyone is around who can help with power tools. I've got your number in my phone now, so I'll be in touch."

The faces continued to look at Mike who was still looking at his phone thoughtfully, hitting keys, a frown on his brow. Neil broke the silence. "That's a bit of luck; let me have that number, Mike, and we'll get a trace on it straight away?"

"Just sent it to your phone." Neil's phone chimed, signalling its arrival.

"He confirmed that he knows that Billy is after him, and asked for help. You heard what I said to him, so he won't be surprised if he spots any of our lads arriving. We just need to make sure that Billy doesn't spot them. What are you thinking, Dave?"

"I could really do with you getting down there, Mike, and I want to be on the ground too. Let's just wait a minute, and see what George has achieved before we rush at this. We still have to come up with a way of getting Billy where we want him."

Neil returned, only having been out of the room for seconds. "That's underway; we should have a definite fix on the area in five minutes or so, and then we'll be able to track its movements five minutes after that. We also now have the plate for the car he fuelled at Wigmore; it's a BMW 320, dark blue or black – we can't tell from the forecourt video."

"Great! Where's George got to?" Dave asked no one in particular, "We can't do much until we know what resource we can get in there, but I don't think we are under time pressure yet." The door opened, and George stood to one side to admit Bob Williams, who had so far been absent from the meeting. He passed a sheet of paper to Neil as George took his seat again.

"Sorry to interrupt, just wanted to tell you that the trace is active; he is where you predicted, Mike, and, at the moment, it's static."

"Thanks, Bob." Neil was holding the paper confirming it.

As Bob left, "What have we got, George?"

"We've got two cars, four up in each, on the road, eta in about an hour and ten, and a second team of six aboard a Lynx, fuelled and ready to go if needed. Instructions are to hold the Lynx team at this stage, because that would be a noisy arrival. The car teams will split and approach on foot from two directions, with the cars continuing past into the village. The two teams of three will then debus, one team to secure the main exit route, the other to approach from the rear. We should start getting some info back soon after 19:30."

"Ok, George, Mike has had a call from Sam, just so you know what Bob was talking about. Mike was right with his guess about Sam's location; we know he is there. Could you shed two of your six man team on the Lynx, and get it up here a bit quick to pick up me and Mike? What's its range without refuelling, and how long to get it here?"

"No need to shed any of the team; it will carry ten at a push. Its range is just over 300 miles, dependent on weather and payload: it will be here, if 'here' is Barton in an hour."

"Set it up then, George, please. You got your gear with you, Mike?"

"Yes, but no tools."

"Can you sort that for us too, George? Can you get your lads to bring us something suitable, beginning with MP?" George nodded, smiled knowingly at Mike, and, again, stood to leave.

"Can you get these car details to your mobile team, George? We've just put a BOLO out for it with an 'observe only' tag?" He passed him the sheet of paper from Bob, and George left. Dave Rogers took the lead again.

"Neil, will you and Phil run the Ops room here? George will patch anything through to us that we need to know. PSR will make any non operational decisions, I'll make all Ops decisions, as things change on the ground. Only Mike will have 2IC ops decision responsibility. Questions? No? Ok, let's go. Mike?"

In the Range Rover, en route to Barton, they got the message that the signal was moving. "What's your assessment, Mike?"

"I'm worried; I can't see Sam leaving there unless something has spooked him. He could, of course, just be going to the pub. What is the tracking telling us? How far has he got?"

"The signal is on the A488, heading North, and is about twelve miles away from the cottage."

"He's not going to the pub then, Dave. I think, at this stage, we need to assume that Billy is ahead of us, and has lifted Sam already. I think we need to tell George to put the team in there now. I don't think we should wait for things to develop. Let's do it, now." Mike was sitting in the back and couldn't hear all the conversation, so had to wait for it to be relayed.

"George says his guys are on foot, and are only minutes away from the cottage, so I've told him to put them straight in, front and back. He'll put them on 'talk through' when they get there."

The chatter on the radio was confused; Dave and Mike strained to hear and make sense of what was going down. They knew better than to interrupt, and waited for the lads on the ground to sort things out. Eventually, it became clear that the approach from the rear had 'gone noisy', when two men climbed simultaneously over each end of the small patio rail, both blaming the other for tripping the line.

The explosion had caused only a slight delay, and a minor injury to the third member of the team, who, although in the centre, was far enough back and protected enough to have only cuts to the right hand, forearm and right cheek (face, not the other place). The front assault team reported that the cottage was clear: lights were on, music playing (now Flatfoot at the Crossroads), no sign of a forced entry, no sign of a struggle. The dark blue BMW was parked at the front under the trees, locked, cold.

"Where is his phone now, Dave?"

"Just a sec." They turned in, through the gates, cursory glance at the driver's ID and they drove over to the heli pad and parked.

"It's north of Shrewsbury now, travelling at about 40mph, still heading towards us. What are you thinking, Mike?"

"I'm thinking that Billy may still have him, and is taking him somewhere that he is more comfortable with. Obviously, he's in a vehicle and not Sam's car, 'cos it's still at the cottage. If he has got Sam, it's because he's got another objective, something other than simply killing him, but I can't quite get my head around what his plan is. I can't understand how Billy got there before we did; he can only have followed him from Cheshire, and that shows how skilled this guy is. It seems to me that he has had the opportunity to 'do' Sam, which, for some reason, he has decided not to take. He had him in a remote location. He had an escape route, and as far as he knew, he was off the radar. I can't quite understand why he hasn't done for Sam. The other thing is that he might have already done him (Sam), dumped him in a ditch, and might be running without knowing that we've got a trace on Sam's phone. I think we need to get the team at the cottage to do a complete sweep of the area – let's see if we can find a body. Get forensics in, and see if we can pick up anything from that. Don't want to be unfeeling about this but …"

"But what?"

"Well, this is about Billy, I hope Sam's ok, but it's Billy we want; Sam has led us to him. It just makes it more important to me that we get him, for Sam's sake. I'm not being cold here; I feel bad about what I've done to Sam – just makes me more determined to nail the bastard."

After five minutes thinking time: "There's no point in us sitting here waiting for the Lynx, Mike, we might as well get back to the Ops room. We'll keep George's team here when they land, get it refuelled, then we can respond when we know where he's going. We really need to get a stop on Billy's car, get a visual on him. We can't afford to lose this phone trace, Mike. We don't even know what he looks like, if we lose it now, he's in the wind."

"We can't stop that car without alerting Billy; it's too great a risk. I think we should let it run, stay as close as we can, but let's not risk anything here: we're too close now to fuck it up by diving in, Dave."

Chapter 44

13th June 1998

"I've got a theory."

Chatter stopped, and there was silence in the Ops room. Dave dumped his file on a desk, dragged a chair next to it, sat, and looked around at the assembled faces, and then back to Mike.

"Go for it, Mike." There was a pause as headphones were removed, and all attention turned to Mike.

"Sam is resourceful, shrewd, and has a background of being in 'difficult' situations. He hasn't rung me again, so I'm guessing that he can't. I'm making a lot of assumptions here, but, on the basis that Billy isn't an idiot, he would not be carrying a live phone if he knew about it. On that basis, I reckon that he doesn't know about it. He doesn't know that Sam has the phone. We are following the phone though; we should not assume that it's Sam we are following; we could equally be following Billy."

"So, why don't we call him and see who answers?"

Focus turned to PSR, who had asked the question. There was a stunned silence, whilst the assembled brains took in the implications of the suggestion. Unusually, Mike was polite (not) and respectful (not) in answering.

"Because, you fucking idiot, that would alert Billy to the fact that Sam had got a fucking phone." There was a collective intake of breaths, waiting for an out-burst from PSR, or an admonishment from Dave. It didn't happen. PSR shrank back into his chair, a brighter shade of red that matched his bow tie, as he realised the stupidity of his suggestion.

Neil cleared his throat, stalling, and diverting attention from PSR: "That makes a lot of sense, Mike, but this is a risky strategy. I guess you are saying we should let Billy run, and see where it leads, rather than going for a hard stop?"

"Yes! That's what I think we should do. I don't see that we are going to be able to take out Billy in a car, on the motorway, without putting Sam in even more shit than we have already dumped him in. Let's not forget that Billy has killed everyone who he sees as responsible for his mother's death. The only one remaining on his list is Sam. He's not done Sam, why? He has had the opportunity to do it, but hasn't. Why? He's got another agenda. What is he doing? We need to know what his plan is. This could actually be bigger than just doing Sam. I've got a really uncomfortable feeling that we are focused on Sam, and are missing what could be a far bigger picture for Billy."

Bob Williams came into the Ops room, all attention turned to him, and away from potential conflict with PSR.

"Sorry to interrupt, but I think we've got a problem with the phone trace. Well, I know we have. We've lost it; M6 North at Knutsford, we think the battery has gone; we lost it between junctions. No way it stopped on the hard-shoulder, unless it was chucked out of the vehicle. Er! Sorry, that's its last known."

"Fuck!" The expletive drew everyone to look towards Mike, but with sympathy and understanding; everyone felt the same.

"Can we track back, look at traffic camera stuff, triangulate phone trace times, and see if we can match any of it to a vehicle? At least then we might have a vehicle lead we can follow?"

"We'll give it a go, Sir, but there's a lot of traffic passing those cameras." The attention had switched to PSR, who had actually made a sensible contribution in an attempt to redeem himself.

"Get the guys on it, Bob, as a priority; drop everything. Let's find this bloody vehicle, quick." Neil said, and Bob left the silent, sombre room.

Chapter 45

14th June 1998

I had a thumping headache, like I'd been on a three day bender. Mouth was full of sawdust, eyes full of gravel, and every muscle hurt. I struggled to try and sit up, and, slowly, my brain started to tell me that my wrists, knees, ankles were fastened together.

There was tape across my mouth – a small hole that I found with my tongue. It was almost blocking my nose too; I began to panic, desperately trying to get air into my lungs. I managed to fight the panic, and get my breathing under some sort of control. It was dark, but cracks of light were coming from gaps around what appeared to be an ill-fitting garage door. I was lying on some sort of carpet, and, as my eyes became accustomed to the darkness, I could make out bike frames and wheels, a filing cabinet and a garden chair.

I could smell decay, oil, damp and neglect. I guessed that it was daytime, but beyond that, I had no idea if it was morning or evening, how long I had been here, or even what day it was. Slowly, the light began to fade, and I guessed that it was evening. I was cold, hungry, but, most of all, needed to drink and to get rid of my headache.

Nothing changed; no sounds from outside – not that I could have shouted for help, anyway. I struggled to try and free myself: arms were secured, and resistant to all efforts to free myself – no improvement in mobility. Thrashing about on the floor had just resulted in exhaustion, and a reinforcement of the futility of it; I might as well reserve what strength I had left for whatever opportunity presented itself later.

Instead, I concentrated on my surroundings, what opportunities might present themselves, what might happen, what would the opening of the door reveal – if the door ever opened.

And then it did. Dark clad, unrecognisable shape, as the door swung up revealing dark night sky and very little else. Nothing was said. He crouched over me, pushed a tube through a gap in the tape, into my mouth, and I sucked hard, swallowing whatever it was, hoping it was just water, but, at that time, the fact that it was liquid was enough. The figure was out of my vision now, but I was aware that he (it) was behind me, and was moving things. There were several trips from the back of the garage to the front, and, although I tried hard to focus, was confused, and unable to understand what was happening.

Still disorientated and spaced-out, I tried to focus, but was aware that giving the impression of being complicit and docile was probably the only way of 'managing' my escape. 'What was in that bottle?' And then the rushing noise was back – I could feel a blackness descending, spreading, surrounding, nothing would move, and my eyes closed.

Time passed; I had a hangover again. A banging head, crap mouth, pain in my back, desperate to stretch, desperate to pee, and then I did. Memory started to return, a chunk at a time, but was mixed and confused with events that seemed both recent and in the distant past. My mind took me from place to place; I was desperate to cling to a thought and pursue it, but it slipped away, only to be replaced by another that seemed random and unconnected.

Slowly, I began to remember the cottage, the quarry, and the confrontation with Billy One. I didn't know where I was, but remembered the dark figure moving things behind me. Was he still here, am I alone in this place? There were no sounds. Would Billy emerge from the blackness? My eyes swivelled into some sort of focus, and I could see that the door was now closed; I guessed that I was alone again.

Struggling against the restraints, I tried to get myself into a sitting position, and ease the pains in my back, neck, arms and knees.

I suddenly stopped. My snorting and panting was matched by other snorting from under the door, in the corner. Then a shout.

"Here!"

Snorting stopped, and I realised it was a curious dog, and, more importantly, its owner.

I squirmed about trying to find something to kick against, to make noise and attract attention. Could this dog walker rescue me, could this be my way out of this? My shouts were just quiet murmurs into the tape, inaudible beyond a distance of two feet. I strained, sweated and shouted, heart pounding – head shaking made no sound.

"Come away, lad".

Snorting resumed, then the sound of footsteps, and the snorting stopped with a low yelp – and it was quiet again. Finally, I made contact with something, kicked against what I think was a bike frame, and it crashed against the door. The footsteps returned, the snorting resumed.

"Anybody there?"

I kicked out again and tried to make contact with anything solid that might make a noise, but couldn't. After an agonising wait, and in the absence of a response, the footsteps again retreated.

It was depressingly quiet then; it seemed like a crushing failure. All that was left was the sound of my own breathing, the exhaustion, a feeling of desolate isolation, loneliness, desperation and the futility of resistance.

I cried.

I think it was at this moment that I gave up and resigned myself to the fact that I would not escape from whatever Billy had planned for me.

My mind was playing tricks, and, for a while, I was back in an Irish pigsty with OB, both of us tied up, beaten up, and waiting to die. The memory of OB freeing himself and taking out our captors spurred me into action, and, with renewed resolve, I gave myself a bollocking, got my breathing back under control, and began to think positively again.

I had a conversation with Mike in my head: "Could really do with a bit of help here, OB; get me out of this, mate, and I'll buy you a pint."

I lay quietly, reserving what little strength I had left for any opportunity that came. There were so many puzzling elements to this; why hadn't he killed me, why had he denied killing Jane, and why deny leaving the crockery? I was confused by it all, but pushed the thoughts away, needing to focus on where I was, and how the hell I was going to survive this bloody mess.

I think I slept for a while – a restless, uncomfortable sleep, interspersed with pictures of the past, and imagined images of the future. I was brought back to reality by the sound of the door opening, with a screech of un-lubricated hinges and metal on metal. I could hear, but not see, movement. A light came on at the rear of the garage. My eyes began to adjust to the change in light, and I could see, now, a van with rear doors open, parked close to the door-way.

Trying not to make it obvious that I was awake, alert and any sort of threat, I moved as carefully as I could to get a better view of what was being moved and why. The shadows changed, and the figure moved, back-lit from the rear of the garage; I could see the movement, although not the figure. The light had partially lit the back of the van outside, which was why I had not seen it immediately when the door was opened.

I lay still as the figure emerged again, carrying boxes, picking his way, carefully, through the debris, past me and loading things into the van. Several trips were made, and, although I didn't know why I did it, I counted fourteen boxes, packages and sacks as the loading continued for what seemed like an hour. The light was switched off – a more careful return, clatter and crash, as he stumbled back with a muffled curse, and the door was closed with a shriek of rusted pivots. I was returned to total darkness.

I heard the clatter of a diesel engine starting, and then slowly receding into the night, leaving only fumes filtering under the door. I explored the inside of my mouth and managed to get my teeth onto the tube which was connected to the long ago emptied bottle that swung around as I shook my head.

If I could get it to swing hard enough perhaps I could smash it and use the broken glass to cut through whatever was securing my arms and wrists. Changing position, I experimented, and managed to get a swing going, only to hear the thud as the bottle hit the carpet. I had to move, but had to avoid trapping the bottle between me and the carpet. As I rolled around, slithered and squirmed across the filthy floor into the corner, I felt the hard corner of my phone digging into my bottom, and was suddenly encouraged, as I realised this may be my salvation. After a lot of strenuous wriggling, I manoeuvred myself into a sort of sitting position, partly leaning against the leg of what appeared to be a work bench.

The bottle was now swinging on the end of the tube, and, jerking my head, got a good rhythm going until the tube came free from the bottle, which skidded away hitting something solid and smashing into pieces some distance from me. I lay back, worn out after my exertions, disappointed that the bottle had smashed so far away from me. Realising that I now had to fight my way across to the corner where the glass had landed, I needed to rest.

Getting my hands onto a piece of the glass was the easy bit; juggling it into a position to use on the layers of tape round my wrists was something else. Face pressed against the concrete, snorting and panting through the tape over my mouth from the effort, I managed to work the edge of the glass into the tape. Straining against the tape, moving the glass back and forth, I cut into the tape, but also my wrists and fingers. I could feel the blood and the stinging from the cuts, but, slowly, the tape began to part; movement became easier, and I persevered.

It was very dark, and I couldn't see anything. My sense of smell and hearing seemed enhanced somehow, to compensate for my lack of vision. The air from under the door was fresh, and as I stopped to recover from my exertions, I was aware of scrabbling noises in various parts of the garage. The air changed; I could smell damp fur and the distinctive odour of sewer, urine and the decay associated with rats. Something moved against my leg, and I swung my legs against it, and the scrabbling stopped.

I lay still, ears straining, and felt the licking at my fingers as they explored the source of the blood smell that had attracted them. Thrashing about and screaming into the tape over my mouth sent them scurrying away, but I knew they would be back. I had lost my grip on the piece of glass with all of this wriggling. I then had to work my way into a position where I could feel around for another piece. I was exhausted, and needed to rest, but had a vision of rats sinking their teeth into my fingers and hands if I slept.

Moving around had actually brought me into contact with a better shard of glass, and I began to make progress with cutting through the tape. I rested, trying to preserve as much energy as I could, and, again, finally, I slept, in spite of my fear of being eaten alive.

Chapter 46

14th June 1998

SIS Officer Philip Stewart-Rae held the floor, and was beginning to launch into a lecture on his opinion of the procedural lapses within the GMP, and failures in communications between them and Security Services, and, well…. the rest of the world really.

George Bennett interrupted: "We have make and partial plate on a car that was parked at your cottage, Mike". All attention in the Ops room turned to him, and PSR sat down with a huffing noise, like a horse snorting.

"The team in Wales has talked to a local man, er!", referring to notes, "A dog walker, who saw two cars parked yesterday evening; one is still there, Sam's BMW, the other was a black VW Golf, and our man reckons that he remembers the Reg. was R455CLA or similar, and he can remember thinking that if it would have been worth more if it had been R455CAL, as in RASSCAL."

"But, 'rascal' isn't double S, George!" PSR, interrupted.

"We know that, Philip. You're missing the point; it's why the witness remembered it, that's all." ('you idiot', he didn't add).

"That narrows it to a couple of thousand cars, but maybe we can get that down to a hundred or so registered in our patch." Neil Maynard said, and then continued "We'll get it circulated, and see what comes up. In the meantime," staring pointedly at PSR, clearly smarting from the earlier criticism of GMP (which he took as a personal attack), "We have established that Sam's credit card was used earlier today in Salford." He paused for effect, but continued to fix PSR with his stare, "He, or at least his card, was used to hire a van. It was substantiated with the use of his driving licence; his passport and a local address were provided. The hire company accepted everything they were given, and have given us all the details. We have established that the address is fictitious, and we are currently looking for the van. Any comments Philip?"

"Er! Well done, Neil, er! Good work. Dave?"

"What do you think, Mike?" Dave said, deferring to Mike, in an attempt to deflect from the obvious animosity that his fellow SIS Officer was generating.

"My best guess is that Billy is using Sam's Card and ID, but I've got nothing beyond that." Mike threw his pen on the table, and leaned back in his chair.

PSR stood, and began pacing about behind the circle of chairs and the wipe board (now covered in notes and almost unintelligible hieroglyphics). The group watched the pacing, all absorbed in thought, waiting for PSR's next outburst.

"What's on your mind, Philip?"

PSR stopped, paused and turned to look at Dave, who had asked the question.

"I'm conscious that we all have different approaches to these situations, which is why we are thrust together, to hopefully reach the right decisions bringing together our varied fields of expertise. I don't want to offend anyone, but…"

"Too fucking late!" Mike muttered too loudly.

PSR resumed pacing, and then stopped dramatically mid-pace, swung to face his audience.

"I have to raise the possibility of complicity between Sam and Billy. Is it possible that they may be working together on this?" He was oblivious to the stunned silence. "They met in Ireland. They met again in England some years later. They were both in the North West. They miraculously met up again in Wales, and now, apparently, are together somewhere in Manchester, and now Sam has hired a van."

Dave was aware of the gathering of papers, and the uncomfortable shuffling; he made eye contact with Mike who, hands on chair arms, was about to press the eject button to propel himself through the Ops room ceiling. He swung back to face PSR.

"I think we have a different operational perspective, Philip. Whilst I (emphasis on the 'I'), understand and accept your view, I think our colleagues, who have worked with Sam over the years, have a better understanding of his motives, associates, agenda and mental state." There was an obvious easing of tension, Dave noted the relaxing slump Mike adopted into his chair, signifying acceptance of the peace-making role that he had adopted. Mike developed new respect for this SIS Field Officer, who he knew and respected as a competent and capable 'hard man' on the streets; he realised he was also the 'diplomat' that he, Mike, would never be.

A knock on the door diverted attention from the huffing PSR, and a dishevelled, and clearly excited, Bob Williams walked into the room. Handing several papers to Neil, he looked around at the expectant faces, and took a deep breath.

"We have a black Golf, matched registration, parked at some lock up garages that are a mile from the van hire company, and, according to a local, it's been there for a couple of days. He also says that he heard noises from a locked garage next to it late yesterday evening."

Glancing at Neil, who nodded in answer to some unasked question, Bob continued: "We've got people looking at the car, and are going into the garage with the landlord. In the meantime, the car is registered to a Nick Pile, with an address in Stockport. We haven't been to the address yet. I thought you would want to decide how to play it."

"Are your guys still at Barton, George?" Dave asked.

"Yes, and the team from Mike's cottage. They can be in Stockport in 30 minutes, if you want them."

"Yes George, but just two teams; we'll keep the chopper team up our sleeves for now. Neil, can you sort out a suitable discrete RV as close as you can to the address, but not too close. Get your team moving, George? Neil, can you prepare your Beat lads for an area cordon, but keep them off the streets for now. I'll only give you ten minutes to quietly clear the immediate area, and then chuck a 300 metre exterior cordon in. Are you doing the background stuff on Mr Pile, Bob?"

"Yes, Dave, we'll let you know what we get. There are two MP5s at the Armoury for you, and an ARV is waiting in the garage." Everyone left the room, stern, determined expressions – all going in different directions.

Chapter 47

14th June 1998

In the commandeered warehouse car park were two ARVs, a military Bomb Disposal truck, and a variety of Police and Ambulance Service vehicles. All were hidden from the main road, behind the warehouse. The uniformed Policeman at the door stepped to one side as Dave and Mike approached. They both now wore vests, carried helmets and semiautomatic MP5s. Mike also had his preferred, holstered Glock 17, all of which had been retrieved from the 'lockbox' that the ARV carried.

Inside, they walked over the sticky 'reception' carpet, and on through a second door into the warehouse itself. It was gloomy: no lights, just lit by fading daylight from the dusty, cobweb festooned windows – too dusty to see through. Although empty of goods, the warehouse retained a strong smell of coffee, which must have been among the many products previously stored. Only empty wooden pallets remained, which had been turned into improvised tables and seats to accommodate the twenty plus men and women that had hurriedly been assembled. Dave laid his MP5 on a pallet, stepped into the semicircle of expectant faces, and waited for the chattering to subside.

"General background to this operation is that we have a suspected Terrorist Cell in a house close by. It is possible that we may be facing a 'hostage' situation, an unknown number of armed terrorists, and possibly explosives in the property." Dave paused, looking around at the now silent group. "Now, regrettably, I would like you all, except the Red and Blue teams, to return to your vehicles, whilst I brief them in detail on the operation. Please keep out of sight from the main road. The GMP Commander will brief you separately on your roles. I hope that you will not be required at all, and I guess you are going to have to put up with a boring few hours." There was a pause, an exchange of puzzled looks, and some disappointment. People began gathering up equipment, and, with some quiet muttering, the majority left the building.

The remaining eight 'black clad' figures settled down to listen intently, as Dave and Mike outlined the assault plan: means of entry, layout of the house, expected resistance, and extraction of any hostages. Because of the size of the property, it was felt that four in the front and four in through the back was too many, Dave explained. The Red Team was to split into two to lead the front assault with Mike, and then two at the rear, with Blue Team held in reserve, also split two front and two back.

The Red Team Leader spoke up: "We expect a forced entry then, unless the doors aren't locked. We'll do simultaneous front and back, only one stun grenade each, otherwise we'll take the fuckin' windows out. Rear assault to take any ground floor x-rays, front assault to go straight for the stairs. You ok with that?"

"It's your show until I get in." Dave replied. "I'll take it over when you have it secure, but, remember, we expect that one of our guys is in there."

"Do we have any better intel on the number of occupants yet?"

Mike, who so far hadn't contributed much, spoke up.

"Preliminaries seem to show nobody is home at the moment, but we are still looking. We have 'eyes on' front and back, and all the regular reports are negative. We've got street-end posts watching traffic. We can't clear the area and put a cordon in yet, because it would deter x-rays from retuning. We would prefer to take them down in the house, or at best, in their own front garden, rather than on the streets."

All heads turned as the door opened to reveal Neil Maynard.

Chapter 48

14th June 1998

Jerked back into reality by being lifted up by the shirt, I was stood up on wobbly legs, leaned forward, and thrown over shoulders like a sack of spuds; I was looking down at the concrete. I was disorientated, but knew what was happening. I was being carried out into the fresh air; it was dawn, almost daylight, but still dark shadows.

My head and back hit the floor of the van, and I looked up at the roof, and then the legs of my handler as he stepped over me. I felt the needle go into my arm, through the tape securing them. Then, dragged to the front of the van, he cut the tape off my arms and legs, stopped momentarily, as he saw the almost shredded tape on my wrists and the bloody fingers. He laughed, and muttered something that I didn't understand. My trousers were removed, and, after standing me up and leaning me against the wall, they were replaced by clean grey ones, along with a matching grey jacket. Trainers and a grey baseball cap completed my new outfit. It was a strange sensation having tape stripped from my face, and I laughed as it took with it most of the three days of stubble. My face was wiped with cool, fragrant tissues, and most of the blood removed from my hands.

I was sitting with my back against the wall of the van, and, again, I felt the phone digging into my bottom. How had he missed it? I thought back, and realised that it had worked its way into my pants with all the recent squirming about that I had done. He began to pile box after box on top of me, some heavy, some not. I had been complicit, not moved, not resisted, had not shown any sign of awareness.

Boxes stopped arriving. The weight of them was not oppressive, and being in the van was much better than being eaten by rats in a filthy garage. The rear door was slammed shut, and I was back into total darkness. I heard the garage door being shut with its now familiar screech, and then silence. A slight movement preceded the starting of the engine – the van then began to move.

I didn't know how long I had until whatever he had injected into me began to take effect, but knew that I wanted to come out the other side with a fighting chance. I started to try and increase blood flow, accelerate this stuff through my system. Limited though I was by the boxes, my movements became more and more limited, and my muscles stopped responding. I expended as much energy as I could. Get this stuff out of me as quickly as I can. I set up a rhythm, laughing at myself trying to dance, bizarrely with 'Sweet Home Alabama' running through my head. And then I slid back into oblivion for a while.

Not aware of which planet we were on, the year, time of day or even the van stopping, it was difficult to focus. Strangely, I knew who I was, knew how I had arrived in this 'situation', and found it quite amusing. I had no fear or concept of danger. The lunatic in charge seemed amiable, and I was quite happy to be helped to my feet, giggling in a deranged, manic and befuddled state. I happily climbed aboard, didn't resist as I was strapped in. My head was spinning, and, although I'd heard that expression a hundred times, for the first time ever, I could see it spinning from the inside. I was unable to control anything, including movement and logical thought. I was aware of a drool of slobber descending from the corner of my mouth, and tried to wipe it away. My hands were resting on my thighs – they wouldn't move. My feet were glued to the floor; no matter how hard I tried, they wouldn't move either.

I was aware now that the van was moving again; buildings passed by, are they moving, or are we? I blinked, shook my head, screwed my eyes tight shut, tried to clench my hands into fists but they wouldn't: 'Focus, think, concentrate'.

Chapter 49

14th June 1998

In the disused warehouse, Neil began by saying that there was still no activity at the house.

"I know you are not going to like this, chaps. The Search Warrant application has been rejected – 'Insufficient Grounds', and we are ordered to stand down." He waited for the explosion, which, to his surprise, was merely a release of air, mainly from Mike. Dave stared at Neil, his mouth opened and then closed again, and there was stunned silence.

"We suspect that the man we are looking for, Billy Conlan, has assumed the identity of a person known as Nick Pile. We are currently talking to Nick Pile's employers; a high security delivery company, Advantage Distribution, based here in Stockport. This company undertake deliveries to banks, government departments and the like. Our man's patch is mainly central Manchester, and includes hospitals, the university and the airport. He rang in sick four days ago, and hasn't been in contact since. He's considered to be a perfect employee – bit of a loner, no real friends in the company. We are still talking to staff, but no one seems to know much about him, even though he's worked there for four years. On the face of it, he's clean – no record, but no history either – which is a bit unusual."

Dave was thinking, and his gaze went from Neil to Mike, and back to Neil. He was amazed by the calm acceptance from Mike, and wondered what he was thinking. "Ok, let's reconvene at the station, and decide on the next move; we're not going to achieve anything here."

"Are you leaving your boys watching the house, Neil?"

"Yes, at least until we rule Nick Pile out, or in. I'll let George Bennett decide where best to hold you guys. Sorry, but thanks for your efforts." Neil turned, and left the deflated men obviously uncomfortable with the news he had delivered. Equipment was gathered, and the men began to leave.

"A minute, Dave." Mike hadn't moved, waiting for the men to drift away. Dave stopped.

"What are you thinking?"

"I'm going to have a look at the house, see what I can find, but you don't need to know anymore. Just leave me some transport, and I'll see you back at the ranch."

Dave paused, gave Mike a long stare, thought carefully and then, with a sigh of resigned acceptance, said: "Keep the Glock, but I'll take the MP5. I'll get a lift with someone and leave you the ARV. Be careful, Mike, this is off the books, and I can't sanction it; I don't even know about it."

Mike sat for several minutes thinking through the options. His thoughts were interrupted by the copper who had been the doorman "Oh! Sorry Sir."

"That's ok, I'm just going. Are you waiting to lock-up?"

"Yes, Sir, if that's OK?"

"Yes, sure." Outside the yard was clear, just the unmarked Range Rover parked in the corner. The window was lowered as he approached.

"I'll be ten minutes or so." There was no reaction, and Mike passed him his vest, belt and helmet, stuffed the Glock into the back of his trousers, pulled his jacket down over it, and walked into the darkness.

The window was raised again, chatter from the radio fading, as he walked away onto the street and around the corner to the alley that led to the rear of the house. The scruffy lad in jeans and leather jacket leaning against the wall nodded a greeting in recognition.

"Just going to have a look around, go and have a fag, I'll be ten minutes." Another nod signified understanding, and a recognition that this 'look around' was not necessarily official.

He applied the first rule of 'breaking and entering', try the bloody door first. He had been embarrassed by that many years before.

The door was locked. The window next to the door was six small panes of glass, and his elbow took out the one nearest to the catch. Reaching in with a gloved hand, he opened the window, and pulled it wide towards him, and, reaching up, took hold of the top of the frame and levered himself in. Standing in the kitchen sink, head bent as it touched the ceiling – crunch of broken glass beneath his feet. He stopped and listened. No sounds. He lowered himself carefully to the floor, scrubbed the glass from his boots on the mat below the sink, shone the torch with two fingers over the lens to minimise the glare, and moved forward.

Living room: clear. Stairs, front bedroom: clear. Bathroom: clear. No one home. Back to the bedroom, and exploration of the drawers and cupboards revealed nothing of interest, but he noted that some were already open, some empty – all signs of a hasty departure. Bathroom again: no razor, no toothbrush, no aftershave 'He's gone', Mike thought.

Living room now: papers on the coffee table, bills, bank statements, drawers pulled out, which seemed to be where the papers were. He folded the papers, and stuffed them into a pocket for bedtime reading, and then the torch lit the pile of clothes, shredded tape and bloody tissues by the front door.

Back to the kitchen – in a drawer found plastic freezer bags, and, as he tore one from the roll, stopped. It triggered a thought, and, on impulse, he looked into the fridge. The light was blinding when he opened the door; it was empty. He shut the door quick before it alerted everyone to his presence. He waited a moment for his night vision to return, then back to the living room, and, lifting it by a corner, he carefully put a bloodstained tissue into the bag. With a last look around, he let himself out through the back door, locking it behind him. He closed the back gate as quietly as he could, and walked casually down the alley.

The scruffy 'layabout', that he knew as Ken, was back at his post after his fictitious fag break. "Had a look around. All seems ok, Ken, but you might want to call in a broken window that I've just noticed. It might be better, though, if you don't spot it for an hour or so."

"I'm looking forward to the drink you owe me." Ken replied, and turned away to study the brick wall that he had been guarding.

Chapter 50

15th June 1998

The van stopped at a barrier.

"Hi, Mate".

"Yeah!"

"Showin' him the ropes."

"Yeah, it's a hire van, not my usual. Do you want to look in the back?"

"Ok!"

"Yeah, know you've seen it all before."

"Got to go! Plane to catch! Ha! Ha! See yer later!"

Nick stopped the van in a gap between an empty luggage trolley train and a 'Service Air' hydraulic platform, underneath the departure lounge windows, towering above. Several planes were on the stands; some being refuelled and cleaned, some awaiting passengers, and some with tugs attached waiting for clearance to taxi.

The van was in the shadows, now late evening darkness. The flashing yellow lights bouncing of the glass above, adding to the confusion and making observation difficult; just what he needed. He released his passenger's seat belt which shot back, the chrome clip hitting the passenger door as it recoiled. Dragging the limp, unresisting body across the seats was a struggle, but he managed, once he had untangled his legs from the gear stick.

Two cable ties joined together around the neck and the driver's seat headrest kept the new driver up-right. Two more secured the driver's left hand to the gear stick, and then two for the right hand on the steering wheel. 'They'll melt and disappear', he thought. Finally, his wallet and credit cards were transferred to the pocket in the hope that surviving remnants would identify the charred remains. Although he guessed there were ten years or so between them, he had a passing resemblance to Sam – had had his hair cut the same, and had grown the beginnings of a beard.

The only remaining Nick Pile identifier was his AVT Security ID Card, which was hung around his neck. This gave him access through the doors to do his deliveries. Leaving the van keys and his house keys in the ignition, he shut the door.

At the rear of the van, he climbed in, checked his watch, and set the timer and the phone trigger. The call to the mobile would start the timer, set now on thirty minutes delay, before sending power to the detonator. He planned to do all that at the departure gate, just before he boarded his flight, and then dump the phone.

He had clothes and identity to change, Check-in to negotiate, then the agonising wait for his flight. So many things could go wrong; he dismissed the thought of a flight delay on the tarmac. Time would be tight from when he made the call. At worst, his plane would be at the end of the runway when the terminal building took off. He thought of the PA message: 'British Airways announce the departure of the entire building', and chuckled. Jumping down, he collected the box (addressed to Manchester Air Traffic Control) from the back of the van, closed the rear door and walked away with the box under his arm. He glanced back at the van when he reached the security door, put his card in the reader, 'Bye, Sam', and pushed as the lock clicked open.

Past the departure gates unchallenged, through the departure lounge and out into the Check-in desk area. He was walking in the opposite direction to the many passengers, and was unimpeded as he sought the refuge of the Check-in area toilets. Opening the box, he removed his 'carry-on' bag containing clothes, Sam's passport, return ticket (although only going one way), to Houari. The box was collapsed and folded, and pushed into a carrier bag, along with the discarded grey uniform and his security card.

Standing on the toilet seat, he pushed up the polystyrene ceiling tile, threw the bag in, and lowered the tile. He expected the bag would be destroyed with everything else in the building. Nick was now Sam Burgess, heading for the sun and sand of Libya. Nick Pile (previously Billy 'One' Conlan), would be the victim of his own explosive device, either prematurely detonated, or a deliberate suicide mission.

He 'Checked-in' at the Algerian Airlines desk, was handed back his passport and boarding card, and was directed to the departure lounges. Picking up his bag, he wandered in the opposite direction, found an empty seat, and waited.

Chapter 51

15th June 1998

"Can you see if we can pick up any DNA from that, Neil?" Mike dropped the plastic bag on the table in front of him, as he walked round to the other side, and sat in the vacant chair next to Dave Rogers. The Ops room had gone quiet when he entered.

"Don't let me interrupt." Mike said, with a hint of sarcasm, conscious that the discussion (of whatever) had ceased when he entered. There was silence, and an uncomfortable exchange of glances amongst the group. "What have I missed?"

PSR began to shuffle papers, Neil seemed about to speak, and then changed his mind. Dave turned to Mike, and leaning forwards with folded arms on the meeting room table and with hunched shoulders, very quietly said: "Things have moved on a bit in the last hour or so, Philip will bring you up to speed with what we know now." PSR leaned back in his chair, looking decidedly uncomfortable, shuffled his papers again, and began.

"We know that a van was hired by..." he stopped, and glanced at Mike. "...hired using Sam's Driving Licence, passport and credit card." Dave sensed a tensioning of muscles in Mike; under the table, he put a restraining hand on Mike's arm, as PSR continued. "The same credit card and passport have now been used to book a flight out of Manchester to Algeria." He leaned forward, put his glasses on, and looked down at his papers. "An AL flight to Houari leaving at 23:40 tonight." Glancing at the clock on the end wall of the Ops room, he continued: "In three hours or so." Again, he paused, looked around at the hostile faces, and, with a deep breath: "We have to face the prospect, unpalatable as it may be, that Sam <u>is</u> somehow involved in all of this, and is about to flee the country. Clearly, we must prevent that, and that must be our focus now." He leaned back in his chair with, what Mike considered to be, a smug expression on his face. Mike could hear him not saying 'I told you so', and detested him even more (if that were possible).

"So, what about our local suspect? Where are we with him? He's not at home, I've just looked. When I last checked the facts, he had lifted Sam from my place in Wales, kept him for two days in a lock up garage, and has now done a runner. We set Sam up for all of this. He had no previous. How the fuck do you jump from him being a hostage to being the perp in one easy movement?" Mike was controlled, but there was no disguising the venom and his contempt for PSR's analysis.

Neil interrupted, he could see that the situation could easily descend into counter productive in-fighting, and wanted to get things back into positive co-operation. "We have a photograph of Nick Pile now from his employers, which we have circulated along with a photo of Sam Burgess." He slid copies of the photos across the table towards Mike, who stopped them with his hand, but let them lie on the table; he was still too incensed to be distracted. Neil continued, not wanting Mike to overstep, say things that he'd regret, but fully understood how he felt.

"We are mindful of how disruptive a major op could, or will, be at Manchester Airport but...", he paused, recognised that Mike had subsided slightly, and went on, "We need to concentrate on the threat that we have here. With the knowledge that one of our targets is suspected of being involved with bomb incidents in the past, it is reasonable to conclude that another attack may be planned at the airport. Previously, these devices have been triggered remotely from a mobile phone. It is possible," He stared hard at Mike, "That Sam is involved in someway that we don't yet understand, therefore, we need to apprehend both of these men to ensure that we don't just go for the wrong one. I'm sure you can see the logic of that, Mike?" Without waiting for a response, he went on: "We are going to put all the resources we have into the airport, with the intention of picking up both our targets to ensure we stop the right one and protect the other. Dave is the lead on all operational issues in this, and I'll leave it to him to say how we now move forward."

"Can we use Red and Blue, George, split them into four teams; one with Mike, one with me, the others in twos?" A nod from George was all that was needed, and Dave continued: "Designation is Red 1, Mike and Red 2 will respond to Mike. I'm Blue – I, with Blue 2 backing me, and Neil's guys will be Green – they will back-up us both, but will primarily secure exits along with Airport Security. I don't want airport lads involved, other than on the perimeter, and I know you will get some resistance to this, but that's how it has to be. Our targets are designated as Nick Pile – 'X-ray' and Sam Burgess – 'Zulu'. Any issues or questions? No? Ok.

Neil, find out if either of our men have checked in yet whilst we are on our way. Our approach will be on the basis that one of them will have done by the time we get there, and, on that basis, Green will secure exit from Departure. Red will sweep from the left to the Departure Gate, and Blue from the right. I don't give a shit what gate the plane is supposed to be going from, get them to announce the departure from a gate that is central, so we converge. You ok with that?"

"Understood! And if neither have checked in?"

"We 'wait out' until one has; it's going to be difficult to take anyone out in a crowded check-in area, and remember, until he checks in and goes through the scanners, he could still be carrying." Dave looked around the room "Let's go and nail this bastard." Chairs were pushed back.

"Oh! Another thing, Mike, make sure your guys know, if you challenge this guy and he goes for his phone, take the head shot; he could trigger something that takes us all out. He has used a phone to trigger devices we have found in the past."

Neil had been on the phone, and, covering the mouthpiece, said: "The inbound flight has landed and it's on stand 16. It's going to be Departure Gate 16, Dave, which is about as central as we can get without cocking up every departure that's scheduled."

"Good, at least we know where we are converging. Let's go, guys."

Chapter 52

15th June 1998

I could smell Avgas, could hear the roar of jet engines, feel the vibrations in the air.

There were flashing, mesmerising yellow lights all around me, vans and strangely shaped trucks scurrying about. I was disorientated; it took a while for things to come into focus, but I was beginning to understand where I was, and who I was. The flashing lights and noise were confusing, and I shook my head repeatedly to try and get some clarity, and understand where I was, and what was going on.

Slowly, things began to come into focus, and my surroundings became apparent. My head shaking made me aware of the restriction round my neck, and I lifted my hand to explore it. My hand wouldn't move, and the limited movement of my head made it difficult to look down at my left hand. Pushing my chin down as far as I could made me choke and cough, but I managed to see that my left hand was cable-tied to the gear lever. It was easier and less painful to see my right hand, which was similarly fastened to the steering wheel.

My memory was returning, and flashes of the recent few days came back. I knew that Billy had put me here, but I couldn't think why. 'Where was he, was he coming back?'

It began to dawn on me that I was secured in this way for a reason, not just to be restrained, but to be secured in a 'driving' position. It was setting a scene for something – clearly, I was to be identified as the driver of this vehicle, but why? Was it going to crash into something? A jet took off with a roar and I realised then, I was in that van... all those bags and boxes in the back. He was going to blow the place up; he was going to blow me up in this bloody van. I didn't know how long I'd been in the van, didn't know how long I'd got, but knew I had to get out somehow.

My feet were free, and I could feel the pedals, but not see them. Looking around as far as my 'necklace' allowed, I desperately looked for a means of escape. Neither of my hands would move very far; the cable ties tight around my right wrist allowed me to wiggle fingers, but that was about all.

My left hand was a bit looser, and, if I strangled myself, I could slide my hand an inch or so down the gear lever to the limit of reach, and back up again, until the ties reached the bottom of the gear knob. Again, reaching as far as I could, cable cutting into my neck, I managed to twist my wrist as far left as I could. Then, gripping the knob with my fingers, tried to unscrew it. It wouldn't budge. I rested, and tried to think of any other means of getting free, and couldn't.

Shutting out the pain from wrist and neck, I pushed the clutch and yanked the gear lever towards me and back, which was either fourth gear or reverse, but it clicked and stayed put. That gave me more freedom of movement. Back to the gear knob again. 'Turn you bastard – turn'. I choked again, as the cable round my neck tightened, swallowed hard, and the cable slipped over my Adams apple, which gave me another half inch of reach. This, combined with anger, frustration, and a fraction more grip, it moved – just a little, or was it imagined. I relaxed for a minute, and then attacked it again – and, yes, it was moving. A frustratingly slow process, a fraction of a turn, but it began to get easier, moving a little more each time. I tried not to think about how much time I'd got, but was determined to get myself free. If I was too late, at least I could tell them I'd tried – not sure who I was going to tell.

It seemed to take forever, but the gear knob wobbled, fell onto the floor, and rolled at my feet. The cable tie snagged twice on the threads as I jerked upwards, then came free easily when I realised that pulling slowly and gently was far more effective. I wanted to rest, but knew I had no idea how much time I had. Searching around, I found the seat belt release, and it sprang free, which gave me more movement. Reaching up with my now free hand, I explored the ties around my neck, and guessed that I was secured to the headrest – I could feel the shiny metal of the supports. I tried to feel for the head rest release, but soon gave up.

I had one hand free, and quickly realised that I was not going to free my neck or my right hand, I needed a knife, and wasn't going to find one. So, abandon that; let's get this van out into the open. All logic told me it was a bomb, and, if it was, I had to get it away from people, out in the open, away from buildings and planes.

First – get it started, reach the keys: 'I wonder why he'd left them anyway?' I couldn't reach them with my left hand, about thirty cm away, arm over the steering wheel, about twenty-five if I went through the steering wheel. Unthreading myself, I wondered if I could move the seat forward enough to shorten the distance, reached down and found the lever. I was careful, thinking that if I jerked the seat forward I might decapitate myself if the ties round my neck were secured to anything behind the headrest. I eased it forward – it wasn't attached; the seat slid easily, and I had the steering wheel in my stomach. I could reach, turned the key and the van leapt forward and stopped. Not reverse then, but still a hand brake to release... and it might be better if you push the seat back so you can turn the steering wheel, 'you idiot – hope no-one saw me'.

Now, not in gear, without the hand brake on, I started it again, and pushed the seat back. Having my neck secured made it difficult to see – couldn't look left or right, and looking straight ahead made me choke. I had managed to put headlights on, and still had the orange beacon flashing on the roof. Steering was difficult, and I knew I had to get moving and get to somewhere away from everyone; I couldn't afford to be stopped and interrogated with a ticking bomb behind me.

First gear, then second, I managed to get from the surrounding vehicles, swerving left and right, avoiding all sorts of obstacles and people, several times nearly breaking my right wrist, as I tried to steer with it attached to the wheel, avoiding moving planes. The clutch wouldn't go down now, gear knob jammed under it. Abandoning attempts to change gear, I floored the accelerator, careering blindly out into the darkness – stuck now in second gear, bouncing off unseen obstacles and signs, me and the engine both screaming.

Chapter 53

15th June 1998

The Dubai bound aircraft manifest showed that it was carrying 526 passengers, 3 flight crew and 21 cabin crew. It was fuelled with 138 tonnes of highly inflammable aviation spirit, about 170 thousand litres, or enough to fill the tanks of 2,800 family cars. The total 'take off' weight was 496 tonnes. In the cockpit of the Lufthansa Jet, the co-pilot clicked the talk button and began the radio conversations, using the strange, but internationally accepted, Air Traffic Control language, and universal abbreviations.

"STO ramp golf, LH 405 requests pushback from position Two Seven."

"LH 405, you're cleared to push."

"Lufthansa 405, cleared to push. Brake released. Steering pin inserted, ready for pushback. And pushing back now, and give me the off-block time, please?"

"Yes, I have that at 25mins past the hour."

"Copy, Two Five and pushing."

"OK"

In the cabin, the passengers were settling back, and the announcements began: "Ladies and gentlemen, we would like to welcome you aboard......" etc etc.

"Ground for cockpit, you can start engines."

The engines start, the roar building, and the interior cabin lights dim.

"Ground for cockpit, you are separated."

"Brakes set. Prepare aircraft for taxi."

"From Ground, confirm all towing equipment removed, steering pins are removed standing by for final disconnect."

"Ground control LH405 request taxi clearance."

"LH 405, cleared for runway 02Right, taxi via Alfa Charlie Foxtrot, hold short of 01 Left. Verify information."

"Taxi Alfa Charlie Foxtrot and hold short of 01 Lima. Have a pleasant evening, Manchester Ground – thank you, bye bye."

Engine throttle levers were pushed half way forward, all four together with one hand, and taxi-ing starts; the huge aircraft began to move forwards now, joining the taxiway, turning past the buildings and flashing lights, joining the line of queuing aircraft, all leaving for exotic, far away places.

"Ok, checks please. Flight controls, Elevator – full down, full up, full left, full right, thank you. Anti-ice off. Pitch-trim – 39.8. Right side is clear."

The lumbering aircraft turns, turns again, and trundles down the taxiway, wings flexing, to point 01Lima, past the sign on the taxiway instructing the aircraft to switch frequency, and now talk to Manchester Tower.

"Take-off checklist. All green. Flaps 1/F, Packs on engines."

"All green Flaps 1/F Packs on engines."

"LH 405, Cross 01 Lima and 01 Romeo and hold short of runway 02Romeo."

"Crossing 01Left and 01Right, and holding short of runway 02Right."

The aircraft stopped by the fence surrounding the vast car park, the lights reflected and twinkling from the wet car roofs and windscreens. An inbound aircraft landed, passing across the front of the jet, tyres squeal and smoke as they hit the tarmac, its engines screaming as it lands, and is put into reverse thrust. It disappears into the distance, more than a mile away in seconds.

"LH 405 cross 01Lima and 01Romeo line up and wait. Traffic will depart to the north from 02Romeo."

"LH 405 cross 01Left and 01Right and wait. Traffic departing north 02Right."

Continuing, now, across the runway that was being used for the landing aircraft, and then a 90 degree turn at the end of the runway, and it stops, runway marker lights stretching forward, seemingly to the horizon.

"LH 405 wind 290 degrees, 13 knots, runway 02Romeo cleared for take-off. Good evening."

"LH 405 wind 290, 13 knots, runway 02Right cleared for take-off. Thank you, Manchester Tower, good evening."

All four engine throttle levers are pushed forwards, the engine noise builds, the plane vibrates, and the brakes are released. The aircraft accelerates rapidly, soon achieving three figures.

"ABORT!" "ABORT!"

Brakes are applied, engines throttled back, and the plane slews slightly right, and then left again, as the pilot desperately tries to slow the aircraft down as the van appears.

It hurtled across the grass, bouncing onto the tarmac, almost airborne itself, back onto the grass, and again onto the tarmac, totally out of control, eventually spinning to a stop, still with the hazard lights on, and with its orange light hanging from its cable, swinging along the side of the van, still flashing.

The plane came to a halt – cabin in darkness, passengers still holding their collective breaths, flight crew beginning to relax their clenched hands, wiping sweaty palms, and giving each other reassuring looks.

The calm, relaxed voice hid the drama: "LH405, Manchester Tower, take off aborted; request removal of suicidal lunatic, and runway obstruction."

"Manchester Tower, Acknowledged LH405, standby."

Chapter 54

15th June 1998

Mike and Dave walked side by side with the others fanned out behind them – six seriously threatening figures. They were met by the Head of Airport Security, who was clearly not impressed by this invasion of his domain. He had taken the phone call from Philip Stewart-Rae, who identified himself as an SIS Officer, acting with direct authority from the Home Secretary. He made the call to the London number that he had been given, and it was confirmed that his 'fullest co-operation' was expected, and would be appreciated. It was polite and restrained, but with a definite, and thinly disguised, threat of removal from office should he obstruct in any way.

Introductions were unnecessary, and he led the men through the security doors, past open-mouthed staff, waving away questions, finally releasing the men into the departure lounge areas. They nodded at the departing security chief and stopped, taking in the scene and the enormity of their task. They were looking for a viciously barbed needle in a constantly moving human haystack. They exchanged looks, and split, Mike taking the left as arranged. He began to slowly work through the duty free shops, bars, cafés, and central seating areas.

"Red 1, Blue 1, do you read?"

"Red 1, receiving".

"Blue 1, check-in confirmed".

Abandoning communication protocols now. Mike had an edge to his voice: "Who's checked in?"

"Blue 1, it's Zulu, over." Mike clicked the 'send' button twice on his radio, which confirmed that he had 'received', not trusting himself at that moment to speak. In his head he shouted every expletive he could think of: 'What are you doing, Sam?'

Passengers were looking at the departure boards, having collected belongings from the trays, putting shoes back on, refastened belts and looking a bit lost and confused.

The men scanned faces, and looked again at the miniaturised photographs they all carried. Walking casually, a little apart, smiling and seemingly relaxed and reassuring, as the excited passengers waited around for their flights to be called. The electronic departure board showed that Flight 889 to Houari had yet to be allocated a Gate.

Passengers stared long and hard at the three, armed men, who wandered (seemingly) without purpose, through the bars and cafés, each with an MP5 across the body pointing at the floor, thumb on the safety catch, forefinger extended along the trigger guard. At least 'Zulu' should be unarmed now, having passed through the security checks, but 'you can never be sure', Mike told himself. More devastating was the potential damage he could do with a mobile phone – much more than with a firearm. What if this was Sam at the departure gate, could he really take him down if he took his phone out? He pushed the thought away, didn't want to dwell on it; he had a job to do.

A sudden rush of static in his earpiece: "Left, bar-stool, leather jacket, lone male, bag on the floor, phone on the table." As Mike moved in the direction indicated, he saw, as the angle of view changed, a face that had no resemblance to the men they were looking for and moved on.

Constantly looking at faces, concentrating on lone travellers, smiling and nodding at the curious. He was looking for the signs – uncomfortable nervousness.

"Blue 1, confirm gate to be announced is 16, over." Again, Mike's response was the two clicks 'received' signal. Glancing at the board – it still showed that the Gate was 'to be allocated'. He was beginning to feel the tension, still outwardly calm and smiling, internally, strung out, eyes darting from face to face, waiting for that glimmer of recognition, ready to react.

The 'bing-bong' of the PA announcement increased the tension even more; his heart rate increased, and the adrenalin rush began. "Air Algeria announces the departure of Flight AL889 to Houari. Would all passengers travelling on this flight to Houari please proceed to Gate 16 and have boarding passes and passports ready for boarding. Flight AL889 is now boarding at Gate 16."

Mike and his two associates were now passing Gate 13 and walked slowly to 16, ahead of the hundred plus passengers who were scheduled to board this flight. Now, standing at the right of Gate 16, with Blue 1 at the left, they watched the passengers approaching from Gates 15 and below, whilst Blue 1 watched passengers approach from Gate 17 and above.

As all the passengers gathered, the seats filled up, and Red and Blue converged and a hurried conversation took place between Mike and Dave.

"I'm under pressure here, Mike! The airline wants to start boarding?"

"He's not here, Dave. Let's let them on, and see if he shows at the last minute." Dave drifted away, and had a quiet word at the gate, and boarding started; First Class passengers, three wheelchair occupants and families with small children at the start. The remaining passengers began to slowly shuffle forward, disappearing into the mouth of the carnivorous walkway. Mike stood back, and watched the approaches to see if Sam appeared at the last minute.

Dave was called to the gate to take a phone call from the security chief, and with Mike's eyes alternating from passengers to Dave, and back to passengers, he waited, recognising something in Dave's expression. He walked towards him as Dave dropped the phone.

"Zulu checked in as a late addition to an Amsterdam flight boarding at Gate 20."

Now on the run, all six headed for Gate 20, scattering the remaining passengers, no longer mindful of avoiding alarming anyone. The 'last call' for passenger Sam Burgess to the Algerian flight came over the PA, as they arrived at the Amsterdam departure gate.

He was towards the rear of the queue. Mike recognised him immediately, saw the resemblance to Sam, but was relieved that it wasn't. Nick Pile, formally Billy Conlan, now travelling as Sam Burgess, sensed the commotion behind him, turned his head to look towards Dave and his team of two, moved away in the opposite direction as casually as he could and stopped, as he was met ten metres away by Mike's fixed stare.

With three armed men behind him, and three in front, he stood still, the other passengers now beginning to panic and scatter, which left him isolated and exposed. Recognising the danger of hitting anyone else in this confined area, including Dave and Blue team, Mike dropped to one knee, and lifted his MP5 onto his shoulder, thumb pushing off the safety, taking careful aim at Billy Conlan. Billy hadn't moved; they continued to lock eyes, Mike waited for the tell-tale sign that he was going for the phone, the twitch, the intake of breath. Or was he going to surrender?

It was a long pause; Billy had his bag in his left hand, and his (actually Sam's) passport and boarding card in the other. Looking back, he was aware that the three behind him had moved left and right. Passengers had scattered, and there was silence. Billy slowly lowered his bag to the floor, and raised his left hand in a gesture of surrender. He turned, and bending slightly towards the bag, he placed the passport on top of the case with his right hand. He stayed in this crouched position momentarily, left arm raised, and, as his jacket obscured his right hand, reached for the inside pocket.

Mike's single shot entered the left side of his neck, just below the jaw, exited above his right ear, and penetrated the ceiling three metres above Dave's head. Billy remained standing for several seconds before, finally, all motive control and brain function lost, he fell across the bag, passport skidding across the tiled floor to land at Mike's feet. His phone, now in his hand, bounced on the floor as his grip on it relaxed.

Chapter 55

15ᵗʰ June 1998

The engine had stalled, and the van had spun to a stop. I was still dizzy and unsure of where I was; I just knew that I was some distance from the buildings that I had driven away from – they were now ahead of me in the distance. The huge jet had passed within feet of the van, and I laughed at the thought of the spectacular ending that we had just missed. 'This wasn't bravery mother; it was stupidity'. It could still happen, though, because I was still confined in this mobile bomb.

Pulling against the cable ties was pointless. I was not going to get out of this. Yellow lights still flashed, and I had visions of faces, reflected in the screen in front of me. 'I do still love you. So sorry!' I thought of a smashed pub window, spilt mushy pea sauce down your skirt, cricket pitches, wasp stings on the bottom, Bigtrack, Fiat 500s, rat up the Christmas tree, wheelchairs, border collies, prize winning flower arrangements… all random thoughts. So, so many regrets.

The van door was yanked open, and, as one door opened, the door on my sentimental memories closed.

Some guy in a florescent jacket grabbed me, and tried to pull me out of the seat, but only as far as the cable ties allowed. Understandably, he thought I was resisting, but I was unable to shout and explain, as he continued to strangle me. I was choking, trying to show him my restraints, trying to tell him to get away from the bomb. Letting go of my arm, he went for the hand that was seemingly gripping the steering wheel, and he realised that I was tethered to it. I could see his confusion and uncertainty, and he hesitated, which enabled me to catch my breath, gulp in some air through my burning throat.

"Cut the fucking ties." I croaked. He left me, momentarily, and then reappeared, cut the ties from my right wrist, and then continued to try and drag me from the seat. My body weight, coupled with his pulling, cut off all access to air and then the blood supply to my brain.

I was aware of the cold, wet grass on my back, the crowd around me, and my desperate efforts to get air into my lungs so that I could speak. "Bomb in the van! Get away! Get away, there's a bomb in the van!"

The airport was on 'lock down'; the van left isolated in the middle of it, no planes leaving, none arriving. Me and my 'rescuers' were in the security building within the cargo terminal, a mile from the passenger terminal. I was still viewed with suspicion; they didn't ask me, and I didn't tell them, my story; too incredible and too difficult for me to explain with any degree of credibility. My rescuers were 'wary' to say the least, but they gave me a mug of tea (five sugars please), whilst we waited for Counter Terrorism Officers to arrive from the main Terminal, and for Bomb Disposal to deal with the van.

I was preoccupied, nursing the damage to my throat, and struggling to swallow the tea. I massaged my wrists, my right having nearly been severed whilst being 'rescued', and, if I'm honest, I was beginning to get a bit disgruntled after all I had been through.

"You guys don't know what shit I've been through to get here." And as I said it, I knew that they didn't even know where 'here' was.

Chapter 56

16th June 1998

The sheep were settling down for the night, the stream was burbling, jackdaws had gone to roost, and the bats were going to be the airborne acrobatic evening entertainment. The new decking, patio furniture, smoking barbeque, and a bottle of brandy each made it easy.

It had been fast paced and traumatic, relating all the history: how we got to this stage. "I'll probably never forgive you, OB, but I do understand why we ended up like this."

Transfer from airport to GMP Manchester, interrogation, intervention by SIS, treatment at MRI, throat stuff, soothing balm for the wrists, collection from A&E by OB in a blacked-out Range Rover.

Now, we were back where it all started (almost); Bleddfa.

"It's a real cliché Sam, but I owe you. So, if you need me, any time in the future, giz a ring. I promise, I will be there. There are only a few people who know what we put you through; what you did to get that van away from the terminal took real guts and bravery."

"No, OB, not bravery." (Are you listening, Mother?)

I did understand the dilemma. I didn't think it was a betrayal, but it was stretching our friendship to the extreme.

I have yet to explain everything to my children, Nick and Hannah, but I may be able to – one day.

Mum died the week before I finished writing this.
x

Dedicated to Ada Annie Williamson
(1920 – 2017)